A KINGDOM KEEPERS NOVEL

THE RETURN

BOOK ONE
DISNEY LANDS

A KINGDOM KEEPERS NOVEL

THE RETURN

BOOK ONE

DISNEY LANDS

RIDLEY PEARSON

DISNEY • HYPERION

Los Angeles   New York

Copyright © 2015 Page One, Inc.

All rights reserved. Published by Disney • Hyperion, an imprint of Disney Book Group. No part of this book may be reproduced or transmitted in any form or by any means, electronic or mechanical, including photocopying, recording, or by any information storage and retrieval system, without written permission from the publisher. For information address Disney • Hyperion, 125 West End Avenue, New York, New York 10023.

Printed in the United States of America

First Hardcover Edition, March 2015
First Paperback Edition, March 2016
10 9 8 7 6 5 4 3 2
FAC-026988-17048
ISBN 978-1-4847-3275-5

Library of Congress Control Number for Hardcover Edition: 2014046203

Visit www.DisneyBooks.com
www.kingdomkeepers.com
www.ridleypearson.com
www.kingdomkeepersinsider.com

DEDICATION

To Wayne McSwain, who for something like forty years worked backstage at the Magic Kingdom, including Splash Mountain, where I met him during a behind-the-scenes research trip. He retired this year, and if it weren't for him there would be no Wayne in the books—but "Fred" instead. (And Wayne is way cooler!) Thanks, Wayne, and the hundreds of others who, day in and day out, are faceless and nameless for the most part, working tirelessly to make the parks and the cruise ships the best experiences ever! *The Return—Disney Lands* is dedicated to all of you!

ACKNOWLEDGMENTS

To the terrific Kingdom Keeper Insiders, thank you for all the hard work! It's another level of fun to write parts of this book with readers of the series, and see their contributions in the book. (Look carefully, you will see them!) Congrats to the few who made it into *The Return*! Well done! (You can see their real names at the end of the book.) I posted some tricky challenges. The number and quality of the submissions was unexpectedly impressive! Please stay with the project at kingdomkeepersinsider.com—and the app.

Thanks to all the Keepers who contributed to the research for *The Return—Disney Lands*. These include: Nick Perkins, who helped inspire the series concept, Brooke Muschott (Keeper Extraordinaire), VIP Guide Katie (Disneyland), VIP Guide Janet (Walt Disney World), and the many Imagineers who have helped me over the years—especially Alex Wright.

Becky Cline and Kevin Kern at Walt Disney Archives who continue to help me dig and delve into archival materials, while Chris Ostrander, Karl Holz, Thomas Schumacher, and myriad other Disney executives smooth the way to allowing me this won-derful exploration of "Everything Disney." I have the best job on earth!

To Wendy Lefkon and Genevieve Gagne-Hawes, thanks for the endless hours of edits through a half dozen full rewrites. Mary Ann Zissimos and Seale Ballenger keep my sorry mug in front of the cameras, while Tim Retzlaff wins me billboards in Downtown Disney and Disney 365s! Without Jen Wood and Nancy Zastrow, I wouldn't know which shoe to tie. Thanks, you two, for keeping the office fires burning and allowing me to write. Thanks to Storey and Paige for helping with social media and to Jessica Kim for the Alliance.

No acknowledgement would be complete without the Allie Lazars of the Keepers world—you, the readers that start the series and never stop, spreading the word, maintaining the excitement, making my hours mean something. To all of you who embrace the series, you are who this is all about.

1

"LADIES AND GENTLEMEN, girls and boys, welcome to the D23 presentation we've all been waiting for! Eight years ago Disney Imagineers, under the direction of Disney Legend Wayne Kresky, came up with an innovative and game-changing alternative to our old friend, Pal Mickey. Five young men and women from Orlando became our first Disney Hosts Interactive, or DHIs. That's also an acronym for Daylight Hologram Imaging! Which gives you a small hint of whom you're about to meet!"

The packed crowd in Ballroom B, Level 3 of the Anaheim Convention Center broke into thunderous applause. The speaker, a man named Joe Garlington, a well-known Disney Imagineer, was like his boss, Bruce Vaughn, considered a Disney celebrity.

"As hologram characters within the parks, these five courageous young people have not only introduced thousands of families to the magic of our attractions, but they've also, as a group, become known to all of us as . . . wait for it . . . the . . ."

Hundreds of people screamed in unison: "Kingdom Keepers!"

Another brace of applause rattled the folding walls separating the line of ballrooms.

"That's right! So please help me give it up to the five people most responsible for saving our beloved Disneyland from outside threats: Finn, Willa, Philby, Maybeck, and Charlene—our company treasure, the Kingdom Keepers!"

The crowd jumped to its feet, cheering and waving, shooting off photos in a blinding explosion of flashing white lights.

The five teens charged up onto the riser and waved back at the crowd. They slipped onto raised stools, grabbing the wireless microphones left there for them.

The interview began in earnest. Finn Whitman, who'd matured from a gawky middle-school boy into a young man with a strong jaw and penetrating eyes, was identified as the leader of the group. Dell Philby, a redhead with a soft British accent who was both a rock climber and a computer whiz, was dubbed the MacGyver of the group, though the old television show reference was lost on many in attendance. The gorgeous blonde, Charlene, received additional applause because she currently starred in a Disney Channel show. By far the most athletic of the five, she answered questions about how some of her more difficult battles with Disney villains had helped lead to the rescue of Disneyland. Terry Maybeck stood slightly over six feet tall, his dreads making him look even taller. He made jokes about being the only African-American of the five, but became uncharacteristically serious when discussing his artist's eye and his tendency to take great personal risks when required. The clear stud of the group, Maybeck received the most screaming from the girls when his short interview concluded.

Willa Angelo spoke softly; Joe had to pry responses from her. She begrudgingly admitted that she'd assumed the role of Philby's high-tech counterpart. Joe also coaxed from her that she'd received a 34 on the ACT, a nearly perfect score, and had earned full scholarship offers from UCLA, Washington University, and Wellesley College. She wouldn't tell the group which she'd accepted, however.

The event lasted a total of fifteen minutes. Another roar of applause sent the Kingdom Keepers off to a greenroom where they would wait before being led to a poster-signing event in the main hall.

Accompanied by a pair of Cast Members, the five cut across a wide concourse on their way to the room. A large gathering of well-wishers and fans already crowded the area, cheering for the Keepers like they were actors or rock stars. Event programs waved; people called out for autographs. The Keepers were happy to oblige, stopping to sign their names or pose for a quick selfie.

During one such photo-op, Finn Whitman caught sight of a girl with dark olive skin and a hint of Asian eyes, squinting with concern. Amanda. He winked at her. But she shook her head vigorously, her eyes darting to her left. Following her gaze, Finn caught sight of Jess, held back by the cluster of fans. No great surprise. The two girls traveled everywhere together. "Two peas in a pod," Maybeck's aunt Bess called them.

Jess waved her arms, clearly signaling *No*. Finn worked to communicate through facial expressions, *What?*

Jess pointed to her head. Amanda made a signal like she was sleeping. Finn understood: Jess had dreamed something bad—a special ability she possessed. Amanda pointed across the hall and shook her head more violently.

Finn and the others were aimed where Amanda was pointing as she called out, "Don't go in there!"

Finn tugged on Philby's shirt. "Not the greenroom."

"Are you kidding me? We stay out here, we'll be eaten alive."

"Amanda and Jess." Finn pointed them out. The crowd took on a life of its own, pushing and surging in the direction of the greenroom's door. The fans knew where the Keepers were headed, and in the process of following them, they were herding the Keepers in that direction.

Amanda and Jess slipped behind the crowd, Amanda looking as if she might cry.

"Seriously," Finn shouted to Philby, "I think Jess dreamed something bad about this."

He won Philby's attention. Jess's dreams were not to be ignored. As Philby stopped short, Finn crashed into him. Finn planted his feet, resisting, but the crowd's will won out.

"This is ugly!" Charlene cried.

The dreaded door swung open.

"We do not want to go in there," Finn said.

"I get it!" Philby said. "But I don't think we have . . ."

The Keepers were pushed into the greenroom. Cast Members fought off the fans and shut the door.

Willa screamed.

A man in a waiter's uniform lay writhing on the floor, green foam oozing from his mouth and nostrils. His eyes were rolled back into his head, showing only the milky white of his eyeballs. He twitched and jerked. A seizure.

Maybeck hollered, "Someone call an ambulance!"

2

THE PARAMEDIC TEAM left the greenroom in a hurry, an oxygen mask held tightly over the face of the unconscious man.

"At least he's alive," Willa said. "He didn't look it at first."

"It's coincidence," said Charlene. "Nothing more."

"Let's hope so," said Philby.

"What? You can't be serious!" Finn objected.

"Don't go all conspiracy theory on us, Whitman," Maybeck said. "Do *not* start with that whole 'Wayne left us a message' thing again."

"He did, but so did Amanda and Jess. Out there in the hall, Amanda tried to stop us from coming in here. Jess knew it was dangerous! Look, we all agreed to figure out the connection between Wayne's watch and Walt's music box. What happened to that idea? Why didn't we see it through?"

"See?" Maybeck raised his voice, angrily. The Keepers occupied a large, round table. He and Willa drank coffee. With the paramedics gone, this was their first opportunity to talk privately.

"Please, Finn, do not blow this thing up to more than it is." Charlene looked at him over the rim of a plastic cup.

"What it is," Finn said loudly, "is tampering. That poison was intended for us!"

The other Keepers scoffed.

"Did you see how big that guy was?" Finn said. "He survived because he didn't eat that much. Anybody want to dig through the trash and eat a whole sandwich, and see how you do?" Finn waited. "Didn't think so. There was only one group of people that food was meant for. Us. This is our greenroom. Think about it."

"The Overtakers are dead, dude," Maybeck said.

"I'm not saying they aren't. But Walt's pen is not in those photos, and not in Jess's sketch of Walt's desk, either."

"That's because if we hadn't found his pen in One Man's Dream, we'd never have redrawn the park with Wayne." Maybeck sounded defensive. "We'd never have saved the park. Solving the Stonecutter's Quill would have been for nothing."

"And my argument was," Willa said, "that the park is whole again, so obviously none of this message stuff matters."

"The park is whole because we fixed it!" Finn cried. "We fixed it using a pen that isn't in the original photos of the attraction. So how did the pen get there?"

No one had an answer.

"You're saying we chase down some recording in Walt's apartment—a recording we don't even know exists." Charlene sighed, and then added, "I have a TV show to shoot, let's not forget."

"I have college coming up," Willa said.

"Imagineering school," Philby said.

Maybeck said proudly, "Art Center."

"You gotta let it go, Finn." Charlene sounded genuinely concerned. "I know Wayne anointed you as his successor. I get how that weighs on you. But seriously, you are obsessed." Her eyes softened. "We just want to help you."

"We're still the Keepers. We'll always have that," Willa said, "but we're moving on."

"Someone tried to poison us," Finn repeated. "Jess saw it coming. That means nothing to you guys?"

"Food poisoning, dude. No worries." Maybeck tried for a joke that didn't land.

"Have any of you considered the alternative?" Finn directed this at Philby. Although the two boys often found themselves on opposite sides of the playing field, they had also figured out how to work well together over the past several years.

"Why don't you tell us?" Willa said.

"Don't act like you're my therapist!" Finn said bitterly. "This is *me*, you guys!"

"You're paranoid," said Maybeck.

"Slightly psycho," said Charlene, "but we love you."

"Seriously, though," Philby said. "What's the alternative?"

Finn moved his attention around the table slowly, meeting each of his friends eye to eye. Then he spoke in a smoky, furtive voice that didn't sound anything like him.

"Why does Wayne leave us a message from the grave? Why did he instruct Wanda to give me his watch with a code on it?"

"You need to grieve, dude. The rest of us have come to terms with losing him."

"Okay. I need to grieve. Note to self. But, *why would he do that?* I'll tell you why! Wayne has been working for years, maybe decades, to figure out *how all of this happened in the first place.* Where did the Overtakers come from? That means he's done all sorts of research. Right? Stop smirking, Maybeck. Hear me out. Philby, after the Disneyland thing, you tried to tell us that the Overtakers were still around."

"I was delusional."

"Maybe. But if it's not the Overtakers, who tried to poison us? I mean, *if* you'll accept for a moment that it wasn't coincidence that food intended only for us nearly killed someone," Finn added sarcastically. "That's a big stretch, I know. But let's say I'm right—as crazy as we all agree I am. Wouldn't that point to someone, as in a human, a living human, who's trying to put an end to us? This is the only time we've been together in public since the final battle. That's coincidence?"

A few seconds of silence overtook the four others. Then they all nodded at once, mumbling, "Yup." "Coincidence." "Of course it is."

"I'm going to say what no one else is going to say." Charlene sounded grim. "And only because I care so much about you, Finn! No other reason than that." She paused for effect. "We're moving on. Our holograms are still in all the parks. We'll live on there until they replace us. Hopefully that'll be a long, long time from now. But the real us . . . We've graduated, Finn. From high school, and from the Kingdom Keepers. The war's over, and you're like one of those guys on a street corner in an army uniform with a cardboard sign. I feel sorry for you, okay? We all do. And that's a creepy, awful way to feel about someone you're so close to."

More heads bobbed. Finn felt about two inches tall. His throat caught. He couldn't speak.

"We need to get to that music box and find whatever Wayne left for us." Finn tried to hide his trembling, but his voice belied his efforts. "We need Walt's pen to end up in One Man's Dream. Without that pen, the parks don't make it."

"Once you let go of this, any one of us is eager to help, at any time," Willa said. "All you have to do, Finn, is reach out. But if you won't listen, what are we supposed to do?"

"And what am I supposed to do if *you* won't listen to *me*?" Finn was almost shouting now. "That guy was foaming at the mouth. He nearly died! That means nothing to you?"

No one spoke. They all looked sad and disappointed.

Finn stood. "Nothing?"

Nothing.

He marched out without looking back.

3

"I KNOW WHAT YOU'RE UP TO," Finn's mother, a former NASA rocket scientist and the smartest person in any room, said, glowering at him from across his bedroom. She drank from a mug of tea, flavored with milk and fake sugar.

"Don't know what you mean." A plane flew loudly overhead.

"Pull down the covers."

"I'd rather not."

"Finn. The Overtakers are defeated. Are you crossing over for fun now? The Imagineers allow that?"

"Don't involve them, please."

"So there *is* something going on!"

"I'm trying to tie up some loose ends."

"That's what I'm supposed to tell your father? He will have your head. You're supposed to be focused on college."

"How exactly does one focus on college, anyway?"

"Don't get smart with me! You know I fight for you at every turn."

It was true. His mother had personally suffered at

the hands of the Overtakers—they'd put her under a malevolent spell that had lasted for weeks. She understood their power and the danger of that power better than anyone outside of Finn and his friends.

"It's got to stop. It did stop."

"Let me ask you something," Finn said. He still had the bedcovers pulled ridiculously high to cover his street clothes, which he wore for the purpose of crossing over. "Do you remember me telling you about Walt's pen? In the Magic Kingdom?"

"Of course."

"Right. Well, we got Walt's pen off his desk from the exhibit inside One Man's Dream."

"The reconstruction of his office. Yes."

"It was in a mug, you know, with pencils and stuff."

"I recall."

"That pen saved the Magic Kingdom, Mom. It saved us. But just recently, we saw the last photographs taken of Walt's desk before his stuff was archived. Warehoused. Years later, these are the exact things installed in One Man's Dream.

"Mom, there's *no pen* in those photographs. It's not there. Plus, before this, Jess dreamed Walt's drawing table. She sketched it out the way she'd dreamed it. You know what her visions mean! Those things come true. Her drawing showed the same mug. Walt's mug. Pencils, ballpoint pens. No fountain pen."

His mother said nothing.

"Wayne wanted us to notice the missing fountain pen, Mom. He wanted us to know it wasn't where it needed to be."

"I think I see where you're going with this."

"Where?" Finn said, meeting her gaze belligerently. "Where am I going?"

"You believe the pen's placement is your responsibility. But how does that make sense, Finn?"

"It doesn't. I know that. Willa and Charlene would be the first to point it out. They say the pen ended up where we found it, so that's that. But you're the rocket scientist. What would Einstein say?"

"What does your becoming a DHI tonight have to do with any of this? Is what you're doing dangerous?" Spoken with a mother's deep concern.

"I don't think so. I don't see how it could be."

"That doesn't sound convincing."

"I appreciate the effort you make with Dad."

"He's worried about you. That's all. He loves you. We just think . . . you're holding on to all this stuff."

"Sounds like the parents have been talking."

"Not just the parents. Your friends are worried about you, too, Finn. I can't condone your crossing over.

14

If it puts you in danger, physical danger, what kind of mother could sign off on that? Especially when it might be for nothing!"

"What about Imagineering school?" Finn said, testing the waters.

"Don't change the subject."

But he felt forced to change the subject. If he allowed the argument to continue, she was going to forbid him from crossing over; and that wasn't an option.

"I could take a gap year," he proposed. "You know how few people are ever offered this chance? No one even *knows* about Imagineering school, not unless they're invited to join. A year, two at most, and I can transfer knowing a lot more about what I want to study. Dad's just jealous because he hates his job."

"That's unkind and uncalled for, Finn, and you know it. I can't believe you'd say that!"

"It's true! He says I earned my full college tuition by being a Kingdom Keeper? Well, that was the deal you and Dad made with Disney, not me."

"I see what you're doing! Changing the subject! Nice try. We're talking about crossing over."

Exasperated, he gave in. "Wayne left me a clue. Me, Mom. Not the others. Me."

"Some say that you're exaggerating that."

"Do you think I am?"

Mrs. Whitman gave her son a long, hard look.

"No," she said.

"Thank you."

"Wayne told you that it was your kingdom now. He should never have said that. You're eighteen. You are not the second coming of Walt Disney. That was the kindness, or maybe the delusion, of a dying man."

"He meant it, Mom. He meant every word."

"You're upset."

"Wow, you're a real mind reader."

"Do not take that tone with me, young man!"

Finn's phone buzzed. He pulled it from the pocket of his pants under the bedcovers.

"Philby's all set. It's time I get to sleep."

"Then I'm going to keep you awake."

"Let me tie up these loose ends, Mom. Please. If I'm going to move on, this is something that has to happen."

"That's the first well-reasoned argument you've made."

"Thank you."

"The pen, Walt's pen, was put into the mug sometime after his office went into storage," she said, as if mulling over what her son had told her. "But before his office came back out as part of One Man's Dream."

"Right. But by who? And why would Wayne think we could help that? Change that? It must have happened thirty years before we were even born."

"You know the answer, Finn. It happened! The pen made it into the exhibit. That makes it a rhetorical question."

"Wayne wants us, me, to identify whoever did it."

"Because whoever added that pen to Walt's desk mug eventually saved the Magic Kingdom," Mrs. Whitman said. Her eyes were far away.

"More importantly: knew the Magic Kingdom would need saving!"

"So I suppose it's Finn to the rescue?" She made him sound like a lunatic.

"Et tu, Bruté?" Finn said.

His mother smiled. "You're quite clever, knowing how I react to you showing off your education."

"Please, Mom."

"This once. And I want a full report."

She switched off the overhead light and closed the door before Finn could thank her.

4

FINN'S DHI HOLOGRAM walked through the back door to Walt Disney's former apartment. The decorations hadn't been changed in forty years. A colorful carpet, a pair of antique chairs, a standing lamp, and two daybeds resplendent with needlepoint pillows. A small round table held the historic glass-domed lamp Walt Disney had once used to announce his presence in the park.

Knowing his time was limited, Finn went directly to the music box. Philby had reluctantly agreed to cross him over—alone—but he'd also expressed his concern; he expected a phone call from Finn every ten minutes so as to ensure Finn's continued safety. Those calls would need to be made from landlines.

Finn worked quickly. The last time they'd crossed over to Walt's apartment, the Keepers had focused on the ballerina music and the unique-looking disc currently on the player. Now Finn opened the glass case and inspected the other twelve discs stored there. Unlike the one on the player, they had all been manufactured by the Music Box Company, and they all looked older than time. They were identical—except for their titles. Finn recognized only one of the songs, "The Star-Spangled Banner." He switched discs to make sure the music on the disc was as labeled. It was.

With the chords of the national anthem plucking out of the music box, Finn kept searching for something to explain the cryptic message Wayne had left him. His mentor had engraved the back of his wristwatch with images and a false address. Then he'd concocted an elaborate plan to pass his watch along to Finn. There had to be a reason. True, the images on the watch had ended up saving Disneyland, but the reasoning behind the false address was still a mystery, one that haunted Wayne's protégé.

Finn scoured the music box for a disguised switch or button to release a hidden drawer. Nothing.

The center drawer remained locked, with no key anywhere. Taking a deep breath, Finn reached his version 1.6 hologram hand through the face of the locked drawer. The tricky part was allowing his hand to go slightly solid in order to feel around, which caused intense, burning pain in his wrist where it made contact with the drawer. The first few tries proved too painful; he yanked his hand back.

On his third try, he worked fast in order to keep the pain to a minimum. He shoved his hand inside; his fingers found the metal tab that locked the drawer, and he rotated it. The drawer unlocked.

Finn withdrew a larger vinyl disc, one that didn't match the others in the set. Its label was marked WK. Wayne Kresky.

His heart pounding with joy and surprise at the discovery, Finn looked around the small apartment and, disc in hand, approached an old gramophone across the room.

It took him a moment to realize that the device wasn't electric. You had to crank a handle on the side. Finn did so, and the gramophone disc played. After a few seconds of crackling static, a man's voice said,

"Match the music to the source.
Ride the tune on a Christmas horse.
Transported now, you're right on course."

Finn played it twice before returning the disc to the drawer, which he locked painfully. He then called Philby from the apartment phone—the first of his required check-ins—and explained his find.

"The label says WK; the voice is scratchy but close to Wayne's. You still think I'm nuts?"

"Hey, I crossed you over. Don't lay that on me!"

"I could use a little support here," Finn said.

"You have more than you know."

"What's that supposed to mean?" Finn asked.

"I convinced Maybeck and Charlene to cross over into MK and check out Wayne's apartment."

"You . . . did . . . not!"

"I didn't tell you because I was afraid they might bail. But they went ahead. Granted, I knew they missed each other, what with Maybeck being in Orlando and Charlie doing that show out west, but for whatever reason, they agreed."

"So you bribed them."

"I found effective motivation. I study physics, Finn. I understand leverage. Call me back in ten minutes. Promise you won't do anything until then."

Philby hung up before Finn had a chance to argue.

5

FOR ALL THE SWAGGER HE DISPLAYED around most girls, Maybeck reverted to acting like a young boy around Charlene, a state she didn't understand. Upon crossing over into Disney World's Magic Kingdom, she had expected a hug, even if between holograms. Maybe a kiss on the cheek.

Instead, Maybeck grabbed her hand and gave her a shoulder bump like two basketball players at center court.

"This is cool, right?" He sounded about twelve. "Having the park to ourselves."

"Right," Charlene said. "Though I don't love the idea of encouraging Finn's fantasies."

"I'm thinking of it as cleaning up loose ends. The guy's been in pieces since Wayne's death. If we can give him a little closure, what's not to like?"

"That might be the kindest thing I've ever heard you say."

"Don't hold it against me. I'm actually just psyched to get a chance to see you. As far as being a hologram goes."

"I miss you, Terry. I miss everyone, but obviously, especially you. The TV show is exciting. Sure it is. But it's also shown me how much you and everyone mean to me."

"Including Finn," Maybeck said.

"Yes. Of course! Including Finn."

With Maybeck in the lead, the two teens climbed the stairs to Wayne's apartment and stepped through the door.

"It's nothing like Walt's place," Maybeck said.

"You want to explain again what we're doing here?"

"Looking for anything that connects this stuff Finn keeps talking about. A diary, maybe."

"Wouldn't it all have been cleared out, given . . . you know, his death?"

"Philby says nothing's been touched. Wayne was important enough that Archives wants to catalog everyth—"

He broke off abruptly.

"What?" Charlene asked. "What do you see?"

"Check out this photo." The dim glow of the thin blue line surrounding Maybeck reflected off the glass in the frame.

"Can we turn on a light, please?"

"Afraid not. It'll be seen from Town Square."

Maybeck stepped back half a stride. "I think I know that photo."

"Disneyland. Opening day," Charlene said. "Nineteen fifty-five."

"I can read," Maybeck snapped.

"It's Walt and Mickey, opening day."

"I got that, too," he said.

"It's so familiar! But why?" She leaned in to look more closely at the photo.

"No idea, but it is for me, too. Can't explain it." Maybeck paused; studied her. "I've missed you."

"I like to hear that kind of thing. It makes me happy, Terry."

"It's more fun with you around," he said. "I'm not saying you should quit the TV gig. Not at all. I'm glad you're happy. But I'm still happier with you here."

"That's sweet, Terry. Really. Thank you."

Maybeck waited. "Sweet?"

"Am I supposed to say the same thing? Look where we are, Terry. Same old, same old."

"I'm accepted at Art Center."

"Right."

"You like it out there."

"I love it out there. I told you, I love the show. The life's a little strange, but it's cool. Complete strangers, kids mostly, know me. They stop me and stuff, but so far it doesn't bother me. I even enjoy it. And it won't last forever. Shows get canceled."

"You've moved on," he said softly.

"Sometimes the tighter you hold on to something, the more it wants to escape."

"Is that right?"

"We're fine, Terry. You and I are fine."

Maybeck turned away from her and rifled through drawers indiscriminately. He searched the contents, some more carefully than others. The small galley kitchen was his first stop. Then an armoire that held mostly Disney DVDs and a workbench/harvest table under the end window that looked out on Town Square.

After a moment, he barked out some words that would have gotten bleeped on Charlene's TV show.

"I don't like cussing. To remind you for the thousandth time," she said.

He didn't appear to hear her. "Check . . . it . . . out!"

"What's that? A saw blade?"

"No way. It's a metal disc with holes punched out of it. Look familiar?"

"Not particularly. I'm not the best with power tools."

"Come on, Charlie. It's one of those music discs, the ones Walt's music box plays. Same size and thickness."

"No. Way." Charlene's jaw dropped. "It's true: you're the one with the artist's eye."

There was a long pause as they looked at each other, then at the disc. Then:

"Wait!" Charlene hissed. "You hear that?"

Footsteps, coming up the outside stairs.

"Dang!" Maybeck said. "There's only one door. We've gotta hide. Don't forget we're version 1.6. That's bad news. No fear, you hear me!"

"Thanks, Terry. That helps."

Maybeck looked for hiding places. There weren't any.

"Wayne invented the DHI technology," Charlene whispered. "Maybe it's plausible he would have models of us, you know, just lying around up here in his apartment."

"I suppose."

"Stay with me!" Charlene spun like a ballerina and focused on two pieces of furniture: an antique television set the size of a washing machine, but with a screen the size of a dinner plate; and a black cabinet with a pair of twin doors on its front. She instructed Maybeck to step his hologram into the black cabinet. "Waist height. Legs to the side, away from those doors in case they open them."

Across the room, Charlene stepped *into* the television console. She lowered herself to waist height and placed her chin in her palms.

Two men, security guards, came through the door. One of them, a short, wiry man, shone a flashlight around, despite the fact that his partner had turned on the lights.

"Whoa! Check out this babe!" he exclaimed, and approached Charlene. "She's like glowing."

"What . . . is . . . it?" the taller man said. He spoke with a British accent.

"Some kind of sculpture." The thin guy reached out to touch Charlene. As his hand passed inside her hologram, he jumped back and nearly fell down.

"No! I know what . . . *who* it is!" the other said. "She's one of Kresky's Kids."

"You think?"

"Absolutely!"

"A holocaust?"

"Hologram, you idiot! Those kids who beat up on Maleficent."

"She's hot."

"Shut it! There's another one." The Brit pointed at Maybeck. "Kresky designed them."

"These are probably stereotypes," the thin guy said.

"Prototypes! Don't you know anything? Kresky invented holograms. Did you know that? And color TV, too."

"Yeah, I heard that, but I don't believe it." The

thin guy bent down to open Maybeck's cabinet.

Charlene's DHI spun suddenly and faced the guards. Her voice sounded nasal; it was a good imitation of Auto-Tune. "Welcome, Ladies and Gentlemen, Boys and Girls!"

One of the guards cursed.

Charlene continued. "You have entered the former residence of Disney Legend Wayne Kresky."

Maybeck spun to his right as robotically as possible. The thin guard stepped back. "Whoa!"

"May we show you around today?" Maybeck asked also in an electronic-sounding voice. "Please feel free to interrupt at any time, and I will be happy to answer your question."

"It's a beautiful day in the Magic Kingdom!" Charlene said, reciting a memorized line from her DHI script.

"Someone should have told us these things were operational!" the thin guy said. "I about had a coronary when that girl started yapping! How much you want to bet this is Mike's doing? Another one of his stinking jokes?"

Charlene spoke in her best tour guide voice. "Wayne Kresky was a Disney Legend, serving as a Disney Imagineer for more than thirty-five years. As a young man, Wayne became personal friends with Walt Disney during the construction of Disneyland. Would you like to hear more about Wayne's friendship with Walt?"

"No!" the guard shouted. "Definitely not!"

Charlene moved her head mechanically side to side.

"Thank you!" she said. "To activate my guide services, please say, 'Hello, Charlene.' To deactivate, please say, 'Good-bye, Charlene.'"

"Good-bye, Charlene."

"Good-bye!"

Maybeck repeated the same lines, word for word.

"Good-bye, Terry."

"Good-bye."

"That was actually kind of amazing," said the thin man.

"Kresky invented all sorts of stuff back in the late fifties and sixties."

"Did he get the patterns for them?"

"Patents, you moron! You mean patents! I heard he got burned. The whole company did. Disney could have made a fortune. Instead, some television company got everything."

"Can you imagine inventing color TV?"

"You couldn't invent the fork if it was on your plate," the Brit said.

"Let's get out of here. These things give me the creeps."

The two guards reached the door. The thin man took one last look at Charlene. "She is some kind of pretty," he said.

"You are nothing short of weird!"

They left, locking the door behind them. After a moment, Maybeck and Charlene stepped out of their cabinets and into the room.

"She is some kind of pretty," Maybeck said, laughing.

"Shut *up*!"

"What they were saying about Wayne's inventions . . . We'd know if any of that was true, right?"

"No clue. I was a model for a DHI, Terry, not a Disney historian. I'm not even a Kingdom Keeper. Not anymore. Philby might know stuff like that. Or Willa. Honestly, I don't care."

"Don't care, or won't care?"

"Look. You find a piece of metal in a drawer, and you tell Philby Wayne was making custom music discs? All that does is fuel Finn's madness."

"We found a connection that makes Finn look a lot less mad than we thought."

"I can't go back, Terry. I have to go forward. I'm a fish with gills, a motorcycle, a bird—I don't do backward."

"We've been treating him like dirt," Maybeck

said. "He's our friend. He doesn't deserve that."

Charlene's hologram couldn't cry—that particular emotion had never been modeled. But her face bunched up, and her eyes squinted. "Oh, Terry! I'm soooo happy to hear you say that." Her voice, too, sounded heavy with tears. "I knew you had feelings in there somewhere! I just knew you could show them!"

"You're mocking me!" Maybeck moved to the phone by Wayne's chair, ready to call Philby and give his report.

"Look. You're going to have to choose whether you have feelings for me or for Finn. The past or the future."

"Can't I have both?" Maybeck said, angry now.

Charlene didn't answer. She moved toward the door and stepped through it, leaving Maybeck alone with the phone in his hand.

6

THE PHONE RANG INSIDE Walt's apartment. Finn snatched it out of its cradle. It was Philby.

"Are you insane?" Finn barked. "Someone could hear!"

Breathless, Philby told him about Maybeck's discovery. "That unmarked disc in the music box means something, Finn. The music it plays . . . We know now that Wayne left that unmarked one that plays the circus tune for us—for you—just like you were saying."

Finn found it hard to breathe. To speak. To think. *Vindicated!*

"'Match the music to its source,'" Philby repeated. "Let's start there. Stay on the phone and play the music box again."

"Stand by."

Finn's excitement took him in and out of all clear 1.6—the state of pure hologram. He switched out the music box discs, storing the national anthem, and playing instead the unmarked disc they'd originally found on the machine. The circus music.

Philby told Finn to hold the phone up to the music

box. After thirty seconds he heard Philby calling across the phone.

Finn brought the receiver back to his ear.

"I Shazamed it," Philby said. "I *matched* it, like Wayne said to do. It comes up as 'Guinevere's Enchantment,' copyright Walt Disney Company."

"Guinevere, as in King Arthur Carrousel," Philby said.

"So I start there: King Arthur Carrousel?"

"He said 'a Christmas horse,' so the carousel makes sense. Maybe I can search that."

"You're as excited as I am. I can hear it in your voice."

"Don't let it go to your head, Finn."

"Maybeck and Charlene helped us out." The act of group participation was maybe better than anything.

"They did. But I'm not sure they will again. We're all moving on."

"You keep saying that."

"Because it's the truth."

"'Ride the tune,'" Finn murmured.

"How long will that music box play when you wind it up?"

"No idea. Pretty long, I think. Long enough to play the whole disc."

"If you're going to 'ride the tune,' then I think you're

going to have to make it to the carousel while the box is still playing that music."

"I can do that."

"You have to find the Christmas horse."

"Trickier."

"And ride it before the music stops back in Walt's apartment."

The boys argued briefly about how long Finn could go without making a check-in call. Philby agreed on a thirty-minute window. Breathless, Finn hurried down an empty Main Street USA, staying in shadow, the faint blue outline from his hologram glowing like a firefly's tail.

Sensing something overhead, he ducked into the Main Street Cinema entrance, peering upward at the night sky. He spotted a smoky shadow against the haze of clouds and froze, unable to forget his encounter six months earlier with a pack of vicious wraiths at the Disney Studios. He couldn't be sure he'd spotted a wraith patrol; he knew the Keepers wouldn't believe him if he said he had. The presence of wraiths would confirm the continued existence of the Overtakers, something no one, not even Finn, would wish upon the Kingdom.

Finn convinced himself that what he'd seen could have been anything.

But as he continued forward past the castle, his attention remained as much on the sky as his surroundings. He liked to think he'd developed a sixth sense when it came to the Overtakers.

If he was right, that sense had just kicked in.

Approaching King Arthur Carrousel, Finn took shelter behind the Sword and the Stone rock.

If he hadn't been a DHI for a number of years, he might not have believed his eyes.

King Arthur Carrousel *was moving*, and *the same melody* from Walt's music box filled the air. As Philby had said, it wasn't the usual one-man-band cymbal crashing, merry-go-round music that played on the ride, but the more circus-sounding tune from Walt's music box.

The park was closed; all the other attractions shut down. Finn surveyed his surroundings for any sign of Overtakers. The sky was empty of disturbing shadows; he detected no movement nearby. Taking a deep breath, he ran and jumped onto the moving carousel.

Slipping through the herd of white horses, Finn looked for anything that screamed *Christmas*. The steeds were adorned in green or red highlights, gold bridles, colorful saddle blankets. He walked against the rotation for two full revolutions, dodging benches, studying which horses were stationary and which moved up and down. His mind stuck on red and green—*Christmas* colors. He looked for bows and ribbons that might suggest a *Christmas* present.

When he began to feel queasy from the constant spinning, Finn tried the technique of focusing on a stationary object far away from him. He picked Pinocchio's Daring Journey and, on the opposite side of the carousel, Mr. Toad's Wild Ride.

During his second fix on Mr. Toad's he spotted a pair of glowing red eyes in the shadows. The carousel moved too fast for him to feel confident about what he'd seen, but the Kingdom Keeper in him went on high alert.

As the carousel slowed and the gears disengaged, as the music's melody slipped lower on the tonal scale, Finn wasted no time, leaping from the moving platform and running for the castle. He checked over his shoulder for whatever—whoever—belonged to the red eyes. Spotting nothing—no one—he wondered if it had been a reflection or a piece of an exit sign.

Back at Walt's apartment, he immediately called Philby. Something was different about the apartment, and the feeling put him even more on edge. He willed Philby to pick up, his palms sweaty against the receiver.

On the fourth unanswered ring, Finn figured out what was different: the music box was silent.

He hung up and slowly approached the device, his stomach turning as much as it had while riding the carousel. King Arthur Carrousel had wound down to a stop just like a music box might.

The phone rang.

Finn dove for it.

Philby said, "Jingle Bells! Christmas! Wiki says the lead horse on the carousel is named Jingles. He was Walt's favorite. For the fiftieth anniversary they painted him solid gold, but now the gold is just on the bells. They run down from the saddle. Shouldn't be hard to find."

"Got it." The carousel had been running when he'd reached it, Finn added, playing the music from Walt's music box. He complimented Philby, describing how the carousel had in fact slowly wound down to a stop, and that returning to the apartment he found the music box had stopped as well.

The line was unusually silent from Philby's end. Typically, he'd have been bragging about his own genius. "Well, if we've learned anything from being DHIs, it's that nothing's impossible. The old Walt dream thing. But, as much as I'd like to take credit for the possibility of a connection between the music box and the carousel, what you're saying seems more than a little far-fetched."

"I know. But it's Wayne, don't forget."

"Agreed."

"There's only one way to test it," Finn proposed.

"You're appealing to my love of deductive scientific reasoning, Finn. I resent that."

"Good."

"And of course, I approve."

"Never doubted you would."

"So, you'll wind up the music box and try again."

"I will."

Finn considered mentioning the possible wraiths and red eyes (or lights) near Mr. Toad's. He considered mentioning how all of that might tie to the food poisoning incident. But he resented being doubted, humiliated, and mocked by the others. He knew to keep his mouth shut. If he didn't, if he pushed too far, Philby might not play along.

* * *

Minutes later, Finn faced the spinning carousel, marveling at its return to full speed. Jumping onto the ride, he hurried through the rows of horses and stopped at the lead prancer. His eyes took in the rows of golden bells, the saddle bearing a golden 50, and an image of Mary Poppins.

Jingles.

Hairs tingled on the back of his neck. He spun and desperately searched the shadows by Mr. Toad's Wild Ride.

The same pair of red eyes stared out at him from the dark. They blinked.

Not an exit sign.

Finn climbed onto Jingles and hugged the horse's neck.

The air went oily. Colors swirled and mixed. Finn felt as if he were being sucked down a drain and was holding on to a rocket at the same time. Clutching to the horse, his cheek pressed to its mane, Finn caught a fleeting glimpse of his wristwatch.

The hands were moving backward.

7

THE WOMAN LOOKED like something from a lame science fair diorama of the Incredibles. She stood erect, like a grown-up Barbie doll wearing a tight-fitting tunic and ski pants. She reminded Finn of a mannequin from a shop window. Her right arm moved mechanically as she moved a glass spoon in a glass pot on a glass stove top.

Finn quickly identified her as an Audio-Animatronic. It suggested he was onstage in a park attraction. Not a first for Finn, but unlike the other times, he had no idea what he was doing here. He couldn't remember crossing over. Had no idea what attraction it was.

A voice came over a public address system, describing the "family of the future." He recognized the expression! That line was used on the Carousel of Progress.

He looked out beyond the stage light. The boys in the audience wore dress shirts with button-down collars; the girls, cardigan sweaters and pleated skirts. Most of the women wore white gloves, while the men had slicked-back hair, clean-shaven faces, ties, and jackets. Not a single tattoo or piercing.

Maybe he'd crossed over onto the set of a movie shoot.

But it was sight of his own hand that caused the panic. It was black-and-white! Incredibly small compared to the Audio-Animatronics. He'd shrunk! Outlined in a thin gray line, he was some kind of corrupted DHI projection. Abort! he thought, having no idea how to return.

The announcer's booming voice continued its spiel—about the marvel of invention and the promise of progress. Finn shielded his eyes from the stage lights and managed another sweeping glimpse of the audience. No matter how hard he searched, he saw only the retro boys and girls.

He reached for the Return he kept in his pocket when crossing over. The Return, which looked a lot like an automobile key fob, was used to shut down Finn's hologram projection and return his consciousness to the sleeping boy in his bed. This, so he could wake up from his DHI state.

Problem: his miniature black-and-white image was two-dimensional, not three. He didn't have pockets. Therefore, no Return. No way back. Another problem: he didn't remember crossing over in the first place.

He ran to his left and smacked into an unseen

barrier. He fell down. Some in the audience laughed. At him?

He jumped and struck his head. "Ow!"

More laughter.

He felt around. He was in some kind of a glass cage. He couldn't make out walls on either side, but something had stopped him. The same thing had happened when he'd tried to touch the top and bottom.

The announcer was still speaking; he referred to the woman Audio-Animatronic as "Mother." She wore her oddly yellow hair carefully trimmed at her shoulders.

Yellow, as in color. The stage lights were color as well. Yet Finn was black-and-white. Why?

Two Audio-Animatronic kids, a boy and a girl, sat on the floor in front of him, staring. Color. Light flickered across their faces, light that seemed to be coming from Finn. The kids dipped their mannequin hands into clear plastic bowls, eating fake popcorn. They were watching television.

Finn was on TV! No, he was *in* the TV! And he wanted out. *Now!*

With skills honed from many adventures in the parks, he sensed something coming at him from his left. A small silver golf ball that looked sort of like a UFO, flying at him fast. It was also black-and-white and in extremely low resolution. If it was a special effect, it was incredibly unspecial.

The UFO shot dashed lines at him. Remarkably, when they hit Finn's arm, the dashes zapped him with little bursts of electricity. They stung! Finn ducked to avoid them. The spaceship altered course. The dashes of stinging pain hit him again.

Wincing, Finn stepped forward—and banged into the glass of the television picture tube. The spaceship zapped him again. *Dang!* Finn turned sideways and stepped toward the glass, leading with the side edge of his image instead of the full plane.

Success. He fell out of the TV's confines and landed on the stage, flat as a sheet of paper.

The audience applauded.

Finn sat up, still flat as a pancake. He was regular size now, no longer miniature.

He vaguely recalled strange sounding music, and looked over his shoulder to see a small television screen in a large box. The flying saucer on the screen was the same one that had shot him. The television threw flickering light down onto the stage.

Although he struggled to understand how it might have happened, he seemed to have come out of that same television.

The show's narrator spoke. "The family of the

future will enjoy television in full color. The kids will be able to record their favorite shows on a videotape."

Finn came to his feet.

The crowd applauded and cheered.

The stage went suddenly dark then, and the narrator's voice cut off mid-word. The house lights came up. A different man spoke over the public address system. "Ladies and gentlemen, girls and boys, this attraction is currently experiencing technical difficulties. Please proceed calmly to the nearest exit, and be sure to return later."

The crowd rose obediently. Mumbling patrons moved quietly toward the exits.

"You there!" The loud male voice belonged to one of two security guards dressed as rent-a-cops with brass Mickey Mouse badges pinned to their uniform shirts. These two were definitely not Audio-Animatronics, definitely not part of the show. They dodged around the stage, heading directly for Finn. Big guys, red in the face and looking hostile.

The guards did not look happy. They were going to want answers Finn didn't have. Like, why was he black-and-white and two-dimensional?

It was then that he saw the boy, a college-aged kid, maybe a few years older, standing calmly at the back of the auditorium. The boy had a penetrating, all-knowing expression on his face. Serene and confident.

With seeming ease, he lifted a poster board sign. And Finn's heart nearly jumped out of his black-and-white chest.

On the sign was drawn a single image.

A large fountain pen.

8

FOR SEVEN YEARS, Finn's life had been as much about conquering his fears as battling Disney villains. As a DHI, crossed over inside the parks, Finn always knew and understood the mission. So why couldn't he remember what he was doing now?

In fact, he couldn't remember a thing about the past few hours. All he had were random, fleeting images and some bizarre music as his signposts.

He remembered stuff like Jess and Amanda being enrolled in the Disney School of Imagineering; that the other Keepers were eager to move on with their lives; that his parents worried about him; that Wayne had been killed while trying to help Finn save the kingdom . . .

But no matter what was really going on, the look of determination on the faces of the two security guards told him he did not want to be caught.

Work with what you're given, he reminded himself.

Currently he didn't have much. He was no Philby when it came to math and science, but he knew his geometry. If two-dimensional, presented from the side he should be nothing but a line. A thin, nearly *nonexistent* line.

He rotated ninety degrees, the approaching men now to his left.

"What the . . . ?" called one of the two guards as he skidded to a stop. "Where'd he go?"

"Gee whillikers! He was right here!" exclaimed the other.

"You check over there. I'll take—" As the man took a step forward, he swore like a sailor.

He'd spotted Finn.

Finn rotated again. The gruff guard reached down and swiped. Finn burst into sparks of black-and-white photons like a scattering of fireflies in the backyard.

A fraction of a second later, Finn's black-and-white shoulder reformed, the sparkling particles coming back together.

He couldn't wait to tell Philby about this!

The guard reached for Finn a second time. Again, a starburst of sparkling light scattered and reassembled. Finn felt mild pain, but the sensation vanished with the reassembly.

The frustrated guard grabbed repeatedly for Finn. But Finn danced out of the man's reach each time the guard tried.

"You don't want to do this," Finn warned in a

high-pitched cartoon voice he didn't recognize. "Joe will have your badge."

"It can speak!"

"Don't know no Joe," the other guard barked.

"Joe Garlington. Him or the head of the Imagineers. Bruce Vaughn."

"Nice try, kid. You mean Mr. Irving. He's the executive in charge."

"Dagnabit, if I don't got the willies," whispered the second guard.

"Because of this?" Finn turned sideways and slipped through the gap separating the two men, silently thanking Mr. MacDonald—his middle school math teacher. Jumping offstage, he fled through the nearest exit.

The boy holding the sign was gone. Outside, Finn passed the Carousel of Progress—and what he saw made his two-dimensional head spin. This place was identical to, and yet unlike the Disneyland he knew. He had little time to reflect on the extra space, the design of the signage. All he knew was that it was Different—with a capital D. Somehow not the Disneyland he knew, while at the same time the park he loved.

As he whirled about, unsure where to go, Finn was struck by it being daytime; typically the Keepers crossed over at night. Also, the park was teeming with people dressed like the audience inside the attraction. Park guests stared; children pointed, their mothers grabbing their arms to correct their impoliteness.

⋊The sky was like a velvet blanket, a beautiful blue. A warm breeze whistled, ruffling his hair in the most pleasant way. There wasn't a cloud to be seen. He took a tentative sniff. The air was light, and dry, carrying all sorts of scents into his nostrils including roasted peanuts and the strangely comforting smell of people. Hairs rose on the back of his neck, and he glanced around.*

It had to be a movie set, but where were the cameras, the lights, the director? And why were the extras swarming the park with no apparent organization at all?

He looked for a pay phone; if Philby had manually crossed him over, then he needed to signal his friend to bring him back. He spotted a bank of three pay phones not far away and ran over to them. He yanked up the receiver before he looked closely. It had a dial tone, but the phone itself had no push buttons, just a spinning dial with holes at the numbers. Of no use to him, Finn thought; the retro pay phone had to be part of a park display.

As he hung up, Finn spotted the boy with the sign across the park walkway. Despite their being separated by crowds, he was fixated on Finn, his eyes alight with

---

*Music_Vision

a penetrating glare. He was in the process of hoisting his sign for a second time—showing off the fountain pen—when he flicked his attention off Finn and onto a Dapper Dan, dressed in a red and white jacket, a straw hat, and pressed white pants. Finn knew the Dapper Dans as typically part of a singing quartet that roamed the parks. The Dapper Dan seemed interested in both the guy with the sign and Finn.

The guy with the sign offered Finn a faint shake of the head. *No,* he was saying. Finn took that to mean don't go near the Dapper Dan, toward whom he looked a second time. Finn had always thought kindly of Dapper Dans; this warning surprised him. When Finn checked back for the guy with the sign, he was gone again.

In the meantime, the Dapper Dan was closing in on him.

Somewhere in the distance, a train whistle blew. Finn cut around the curving outside of the Carousel of Progress, hoping to catch the Disneyland Railroad, but the train had pulled out of the station. Worse yet, he was beginning to attract a following of the curious. And there, in the distance, still pursuing him, the Dapper Dan.

Finn pulled on a door handle on the exterior of the huge pavilion housing the Carousel of Progress.

Locked. Another, also locked. Forced to move in the direction of the approaching Dapper Dan in order to keep testing doors, he hurried now, tendrils of panic choking his nerves. Locked. Locked.

Unexpectedly, a door burst open and swung through the black-and-white Finn, dispersing his pixels like confetti. People wearing the same retro costumes flowed out the door. Finn's image reassembled, and he hurried inside. Each time a person bumped him, he exploded into the same dustlike pixels. This effect impeded his progress; the pixels had to re-form into his image before Finn could move again.

The Dapper Dan's striped jacket and white pants moved against the outgoing tide, coming for Finn.

Finn dodged through the human pylons as if in a video game, trying to avoid being delayed by pixelization. Inside the same auditorium as before, he hurried toward the stage.

"You!" The Dapper Dan was close now.

Onstage, Finn panicked. He was life-size; the TV screen, tiny. When he led with his open palm, the picture tube's glass proved an unbreakable barrier; his hand slapped uselessly against it. He tried his fingertips, like a jab. Now his projected hand went through the glass and shrank to a tenth of its size.

The Dapper Dan charged up the stage stairs.

Finn pulled his hand out. He knew that all things DHI required trust. It had been one of the early lessons Wayne had taught them. Crossing over was as much about one's belief as it was about photons and high-data projection systems. Fear was a 1.6 DHI's undoing. Confidence, his mainstay. If a geometric plane, his projection would strike the glass; if a line—the edge of that plane—it would pass through. *Thank you, Mr. MacDonald!*

He had no choice. With the Dapper Dan nearly upon him, Finn hurried back several steps, took a running start, and raced toward the glowing television. He leaped and dived, hands together like he was diving into a swimming pool. He expected a collision, the sound of breaking glass, sparks, and possibly a fire.

Instead, his vision went oily for the second time. He thought he heard the Dapper Dan screaming, but the man's words were indecipherable. Somehow, they sounded almost as if they were playing at fast-forward.

9

FINN BLINKED THROUGH blurred vision. When it cleared, he found himself riding Jingles on King Arthur Carrousel. He confirmed his status as a hologram by running his hand through the brass supporting Jingles.

He didn't remember anything beyond climbing onto the horse. Though his arm stung and it felt as if he'd lost time, a few minutes perhaps, he was disappointed that nothing had happened. In fact, he felt like a fool for believing something would. He glanced at his watch, feeling drawn to it. It was late, but it was nearly always late when he returned.

Climbing down off Jingles, Finn caught sight of a scar on his right forearm. He leaned in for a closer look.

It wasn't a scar, but a crude sketch of a missile. No, not a missile, but a . . . pen. A fountain pen, just like Walt's.

Unable to remember how the pen got onto his arm, he stood on the carousel, watching the park spin past, perplexed. He felt a little like he had the time he'd slipped while running around the rec center swimming pool and thumping his head on the concrete. Dazed.

Coming out of that daze he recalled the red eyes glowing in the shadows. He ducked behind the horses, and crawled on hands and knees to the outer edge of the carousel. He slipped off onto the asphalt, and started running.

Racing through the dark park and around the castle, his imagination went wild. He could picture whatever creature belonged to those red eyes coming after him. He could envision the wraiths swirling overhead, descending, shrieking with anger.

At last, he reached the Partners statue and, with the Return in hand, pushed the button.

10

FINN SAT BOLT UPRIGHT IN BED and peeled away the bedding to reveal he was wearing street clothes. He had a series of red blotches on his left arm, like bee stings.

Taking a deep breath, he yanked his right shirt sleeve to his elbow.

A fountain pen was drawn on his arm.

"Well?"

He jumped, practically levitating off the mattress.

"Mom?" He pulled down his sleeve.

"You were expecting someone else?" she said. She sat on his desk chair in her nightgown and robe.

"I was expecting you to be in your bed sleeping."

"Sorry to disappoint," she said.

"You scared me."

"I don't think you needed me for that. You looked plenty scared when you came awake." She crossed the robe tighter at her neck as if chilly. The room was warm. "Are you going to tell me about your arm?"

Finn held out his forearm, hoisted his sleeve once again, and turned on the bedside light. He said nothing.

"So?"

"No big deal."

"Walt's pen?" his mother asked. "Looks like that to me."

Finn withdrew Walt's pen from his pocket and held it up for comparison. "Pretty close, I'd say."

"And?"

"And I didn't draw it, Mom. I'm not much as a lefty."

She sat on the bed beside him, looked again at his forearm.

"First of all," Finn said, "the only pen I have on me is Walt's fountain pen, and this drawing isn't fountain pen ink. It's from a ballpoint or some kind of marker."

"Mmmm," she said, inspecting the sketch more closely.

"And like I said, it's on my right arm, meaning I would have drawn it with my left. I can't draw stick figures with my left hand, much less something as good as this."

He jumped out of bed. Checked his watch. "I've got to call Philby and let him know I returned."

She sat there, unmoving. "Go ahead."

"Alone, Mom. In private."

"Because?"

"I appreciate the concern, really. But I'm back. I'm

fine. And I'm not going anywhere. I'll see you in the morning." Finn reached out to open his bedroom door. Light from the hallway winked off the face of his wristwatch.

"Mom, what's the date?"

"Right now?"

"Right now. Today."

"The eighth."

"Not the seventh? You're sure?"

"Positive. Why?"

Finn tapped his wristwatch's crystal face. "This thing's busted. It's saying the seventh. It's eleven thirty-nine, right?"

"Two thirty. We can get it looked at."

"Two thirty! Maybe . . . yeah, whatever." He looked to the open door. "Please? We should both be asleep."

Mrs. Whitman swooshed out of the bedroom, her robe wafting behind her like a queen's cloak.

11

"It's two thirty, man. I'm sleeping. Or I was." Philby sounded groggy.

"I returned."

"Yes. Congratulations. And I went to bed the moment I saw the data spike indicating you had."

"Like five minutes ago," Finn said. "It's not as if I've cost you a lot of sleep."

"Whatever."

"I was on King Arthur Carrousel. On Jingles."

"I think I knew that."

"But when I got off, Walt's pen was drawn on my arm."

"Drawn by whom?"

"You sound like my mother."

"Answer the question."

"Not me. I didn't see anyone else."

"That's impossible."

"Which is, in part, why I'm calling you."

"We don't fall asleep as DHIs. Not ever. It's not as if you nodded off and someone drew on you while you were sleeping. Text me a photo."

Finn did. He heard Philby's phone ding and said, "Check out the ink. The only pen I had on me was the fountain pen. But that pen is drawn in—"

"Ballpoint or marker."

"Exactly what I told my mother!"

"Your mother?"

"Long story. Later. Look, I didn't draw it, and I didn't have a pen to draw it with."

"What about it being drawn on your other self? Your sleeping self?"

"Impossible. My mother was watching me."

"You have issues."

"Tell me about it."

"Walk me through your time in the park. Tell me what you remember."

"Zero. I remember climbing onto Jingles and climbing off. Hey! What if this is like *Insidious* or something?"

"*Inception*," Philby corrected. "You mean *Inception*. Layers of sleep, layers of consciousness, right?"

"Right, yes."

Philby breathed heavily into the phone. "You seriously think you entered a wormhole and someone drew on your arm?"

"What's a wormhole? No, I think I blacked out on Jingles. I think someone came along and drew on my arm, maybe as a message. A clue."

"And you want me to suggest this to the others? They've already got one foot out the door, Finn. You know that."

"So how did it get there?"

"No clue. A software glitch might explain the memory loss, but not the pen. You must remember something."

"I wish."

"Climbing on and off Jingles. That's it?"

"My watch messed up. It's still running, but it's a few hours off."

"When you want to start making sense, I'm listening."

"You know what?" Finn fished an image from his subconscious; felt dizzy, dazed. "When I was on Jingles . . . I remember holding on—to his neck, you know? Because I was getting dizzy. I couldn't see straight. Everything was . . . blurry. But I remember my watch. I think the hands were moving backward."

"Say again."

"It makes no sense, or maybe it does, since the date on my watch never advanced. You know how your phone resets the time to the current time zone? I think my watch did that. All on its own."

"But it's just a regular watch, right? Not an Apple Watch or something?"

"Regular old, cheap watch. A Timex. The thing has never once had a problem."

"Except for moving backward?"

"Obviously that didn't happen, but that's what I saw."

"Slow or fast?"

"What? The hands?"

"The hands were moving slow or fast?" Philby asked.

"I dreamed it, Philby. Obviously! It supports my losing consciousness. They moved fast. I'm telling you, I blacked out. I think an Overtaker drew that pen on my arm."

"What Overtaker? They're gone, Finn."

"Look, I know what you guys think of me, Philby. It doesn't take a genius to know when you're being mocked and teased. If you guys weren't such good friends, it wouldn't hurt so much, but you are. Good friends, I mean. But I saw what I saw. I have a pen drawn on my arm. Something happened when I was on that horse. I have no idea what. But it happened, and if you had an ounce of kindness in you, you'd cross me back over and let me try it again. Knowing you, though, that won't happen, so you're stuck with crazy Finn and his crazy drawing on his arm."

"Are you quite done?" When Philby's temper

showed, his years in England changed his accent and his phrasing.

"I guess. Yeah."

"The hands of your watch went backward. *Quickly.* You're sure of that?"

"Yes."

"You felt dizzy."

"I said so. Yes."

"You remember nothing until you found yourself back on Jingles, but now you have a drawing on your arm?" Philby paused for a long moment. "Finn, have you ever read Jules Verne?"

"Never."

"Do you know that Walt Disney loved his work? *Twenty Thousand Leagues Under the Sea*, for one."

"I think I could have guessed as much."

"He most likely appreciated H. G. Wells, too."

"Where are you going with this, Philby?"

"It's not a question of where I'm going, Finn. It's a question of where you've been." Philby paused the way he did when his tongue couldn't catch up with his thoughts. Slowly, as if afraid to speak, he quoted the words Wayne Kresky had spoken before he'd been killed.

"'It's about time.'"

ANAHEIM, CALIFORNIA

Disney School of Imagineering

12

"PHILBY CALLED," AMANDA told Jess across a lunch table bearing two orange trays from the Team Disney commissary. As they spoke, Jess squeezed a piece of packaged California roll between disposable chopsticks; Amanda wolfed down penne pasta with rotisserie chicken and Parmesan.

"And?" Jess asked, knowing by Amanda's tone that it was something important to the Keepers—and nothing personal. If it were personal, Finn would have been the one to call Amanda.

"He needs our help. It's for Finn, he said. Research."

"Spying?"

"I don't know exactly." Amanda shook her head, brow furrowed in confusion. "He wants me—us?—to dig into the early work of the Imagineers' involvement with television. He says it's not stuff the Archives would have. But he thinks we'll find it here. White papers, they're called."

Here was the Disney School of Imagineering, which operated out of the Team Disney building, located just behind a towering wall separating a backstage area from Disneyland's Toontown. Few of the Team Disney Cast Members knew of the school's existence. It had its own entrance, and the college-age students coming and going were easily mistaken for Cast Members. Those familiar with the school called it "DSI."

Enrollment at DSI hovered around one hundred and fifty. DSI students ate lunch in two shifts in their own commissary.

Amanda Lockhart and Jess Lockhart, two of the newly enrolled students, were sometimes thought to be sisters despite their differing looks. Amanda, olive-skinned and vaguely Asian around the eyes, stood five-foot-eight and was full figured. Jess's complexion was pale. Her white hair (not blond), made her witch-like and odd. She could have used a few inches and a few pounds. Both pretty in their own right, the two girls carried an air of mystery and beguiling self-confidence. They'd learned the art of survival at an early age. Jessica, who had no clear birth identity, had adopted Amanda's last name after the two escaped a secure research facility that pretended to be a boarding school. There they'd been used as guinea pigs by a shadowy organization interested in their unusual "gifts." Barracks 14, as its young residents referred to the research facility, had been the worst and scariest years— ever. Getting out had been the best thing either girl had accomplished. Staying out remained a challenge.

A few key Imagineers knew about the girls' past at Barracks 14. They had negotiated Jess's and Amanda's current enrollment in DSI, and were helping keep their location confidential.

"Philby needs the full history of television in the park and in the company," Amanda said now. The more fiery of the two, she displayed great passion for things that interested her and paid little attention to the rest. She'd helped the Kingdom Keepers rescue Jess from the clutches of Maleficent by deploying her "special talent," telekinesis. She could physically move almost anything without touching it. A simple "push" of her arms, driven by a focused intention—anger, fear, hatred—and she could move chairs, close doors, break windows.

"Well, at least he's not asking for much," snapped Jess, emitting a high-pitched hiss like a tire losing air. "The full history of TV? That sounds like a PhD thesis."

"Philby says the Imagineers keep a stash of files off-site in the dorm. It's the stuff they don't want students to find or others to see. Old exams. Legal stuff."

"What happened to him coming here himself? He's already been accepted. He can do it in a couple weeks."

"I think it's about timing at this point. He needs us. Finn needs us."

"Mandy, I wouldn't trade our time with the Keepers for anything. You know that. But it's over. I'm not going to keep battling villains that don't exist anymore. Finn . . . since Wayne . . . he's paranoid. He has issues, Mandy. This kind of thing is not going to help."

Amanda sat back in her chair, set down her fork. Jess knew her well enough to see she was withdrawing into herself. "He needs me," she said softly.

"I like it here. I'd like to stay enrolled."

"It's Philby asking, not Finn. Doesn't that mean anything to you?"

"Of course it does. But this school is by far the coolest thing we've ever done, or ever could do. Wrap your mind around that: we're being paid to learn about all the coolest stuff Disney has ever done. Why risk it?"

"Wrap your mind around this: why are you and I students here? Because we helped the Keepers. Because we're their friends. And because of them, we happen to know a lot of important people in the company. That's why we were offered this in the first place."

"I just . . . I don't want to be the oddball anymore," Jess said, her voice growing soft. "We've been called witches, spooks, freaks, and aliens. I'm not naive, Mandy—the other students here will eventually realize what we can do. But I don't want to do anything— anything!—to make that happen faster. I want to just start over as a normal girl. We've talked about this, Mandy. You want it as much as I do."

"I do," Amanda confessed. "It's true. I want all that and more. Friendships that last. A room I can actually call mine—ours! A chance to go to movies and malls and do the stuff we've never done."

"DSI is going to make that stuff happen."

Amanda nodded, though sadly.

"One phone call from Philby changes that?"

Amanda's pained expression cut at Jess like a knife. "He needs us, Jess. He saved you. Now we've got to save him."

"Do not guilt-trip me."

"They found a message in Wayne's apartment. Finn crossed over and weird things happened to him. Philby won't say exactly what, but he obviously thinks it has to do with the Imagineers' early experiments with television. It's a couple of folders. That's all he needs."

"I will not get myself expelled, even for Philby or Finn."

"He's our friend."

"Of course he is! I'm not arguing that. I love them all. Really. As in, love them. Finn, too. But you're in deep with him, way too deep. We're moving on here, Mandy. I'm not saying we can't have them as friends. That's always and forever. But we can't risk this chance that's been given to us. We jumped ahead of thousands of kids on a list. Kids who would do anything to be Imagineers. Do not mess this up."

"Philby said Becky Cline told him about the Imagineer stuff. She mentioned the dorm library."

"The Tower library?" Jess sat back, her face thoughtful. "That's different. That's a public space. Getting in there is no problem."

"That's all I'm saying."

"You know it's not. It always starts with something like this," Jess said. "Right? A message. A clue. And it gets out of hand. I'm not going there. I will not lose this chance."

"We're not going to take anything. We're not going to steal or . . . whatever. We're just going to look around for a couple of books in the library."

An older girl crossed the commissary, heading toward them at a brisk pace. Both girls took notice. Her dark hair was pulled back tightly, stretching skin riddled with acne.

"Which one's Amanda?" the girl asked, giving them a bright smile.

Amanda raised her hand cautiously.

"Peggy wants to see you."

"Peggy?"

"Victoria Llewelyn. Don't ask me why she's called Peggy! She's the first year adviser. All first years get reviewed. It's kinda random when it happens. You'll like her."

Amanda looked over at Jess. Her eyes said, *Please*.

Jess nodded, but a frown contorted her face.

13

"I DON'T MEAN TO BE RUDE, but I thought I'd already been accepted into the program." Amanda took in the officious looking, cinnamon-skinned woman sitting before her. Peggy had soft jowls, a high hairline, and a lovely Caribbean accent. The well-lit office, with its rainbow colored carpet squares and a stainless steel and glass desk, was personalized with a custom monthly wall calendar showing either grandchildren or nieces and nephews on a playground. A Magic 8-Ball and a row of five trophies of faux-bronzed knitting needles and plastic yarn balls occupied an oddly placed half-length shelf.

The back of Peggy's computer terminal had been dusted recently; the wires, gathered in colorful plastic ties reminiscent of a horsetail braid, ran to the floor, where they stretched toward outlets and other connected gear.

"We conduct periodic reviews." Peggy had a voice like a bass fiddle.

"It's so soon, though."

"Some of our students show early promise."

"You're just saying that, right?"

"Don't you think you're doing well?" She clicked her mechanical pencil absentmindedly. It hovered threateningly over a legal pad on a slanted binder; the angle prevented Amanda from seeing what Peggy was writing.

"I guess I'm doing all right."

"You have an unusual ability," Peggy said. "Have you used it since you joined us?"

"No!"

"Why not?"

"Excuse me?"

"Why haven't you used your gift? This is a program for the gifted."

"Not my kind of gifted," Amanda said.

"Because?"

"Does it say somewhere in there what I do?" Amanda asked. "Because I don't think you'd say that if you knew."

"Are you embarrassed by your telekinetic powers?"

Amanda swallowed dryly. The woman knew! "Look, when I was ten, I slammed a door without touching it. After that, I could move couches. Dressers. Chairs with people sitting in them. I was living with an unmarried aunt who couldn't 'handle me.' That year, I was sent to a 'school'"—she drew the air quotes—"that just happened to get regular visits from people in suits and uniforms.

There was no talk of our rights. They made me perform like a circus animal. Embarrassed? Sure. Humiliated. Afraid of myself and what I might do by accident. I've learned to control my gift, but it's really hard sometimes. I've tried meditation, prayer, you name it. The point being: I'm trying to stop. I'm trying to blend in for a change."

"We don't hire those who blend in, Amanda. We hire those who stand out."

"O . . . kay. So that means . . . ?"

"Be yourself. The real you. Nothing more. Don't hide. That's all we ask."

"I break things." Amanda sat forward, her hands clenched tightly between her knees. She met Peggy's eyes, trying to convince her, to make her see. "I can hurt people."

"You are as unique as any of our students. No more, no less."

"That would be a first."

"Believe it. We have young painters, audio technicians, creative thinkers, dietitians, performers . . . even a telekinetic." Peggy smiled. Amanda also caught herself grinning.

"And women who are very good at winning the confidence of girls who sit across from them. Psychologist?"

Peggy's eyes sparkled. "And girls who are practiced

in turning the conversation away from themselves."

"There's been no reason," Amanda said. "To move things. I call it *pushing*. But I don't need to push. I feel safe here in Imagineering school."

"You shouldn't," Peggy said calmly. "Of the one hundred and thirty-seven students enrolled this semester, less than half will eventually be invited to work with the Imagineers. Fewer than twenty will join more elite departments."

"What?" Amanda felt the icy sting of shock. She and Jess could be dropped before they'd even really begun? "We haven't been told any of this."

"I'm telling you now. I ask you not to broadcast it."

"But why? To scare me? 'Cause you're doing a decent job of that."

"It's not my intention, I assure you. This is meant to be motivation."

"Because I'm a freak, and you want to determine if the freak can control herself."

"I hope you don't believe that." The woman's total conviction had won Amanda's attention, slipped right past her careful defenses. "A person with unusual abilities is not an unusual person. Don't confuse the two. We, all of us, have individual talents. Some we share. Some we hide. I'm telling you—as I will tell the others with high aptitude—that certain opportunities are limited. Don't hide your talents. We have a song in the stage adaptation of Mary Poppins about reaching for the stars. I suggest you download it."

"You know everything about me," Amanda said. "I just realized that."

"I wouldn't go that far."

"You're trying to help me." Peggy nodded. Amanda's voice dropped almost to a whisper. "Thank you. But what if the me you're trying to help doesn't love the me that has to do with my 'talent'?"

"What you and Jessica have been through has matured you well beyond others your age." Peggy sat back at her desk, carefully considering Amanda. "Your experiences qualify you uniquely for our advanced placement track. It's my job to let you know these opportunities are yours for the taking. I won't try to sell you one way or the other. Each of us must weigh our own worth—to others, and to ourselves."

She leaned in slightly. Amanda took a deep breath. It felt as if there was very little air in the room.

"I can see you don't fully trust me," Peggy said softly. "I'd like to work with you on that."

"It's not just you, if that's any consolation. In my experience, grown-ups and guardians tend to say one thing and do another. I believe it's called hypocrisy."

"A lack of moral fiber. I would venture to say you

won't find that here. Not in the company as a whole, and certainly not in the Imagineers. The company, the Kingdom as you and your friends call it, is in our hands. The direction, the future of the stories we tell in our parks. It's a huge responsibility. Do we always get it right? No. But that's why new blood, new minds are so important to our longevity."

"I'm hoping the blood part is behind us. We lost a friend, you know." Amanda's voice caught, remembering Finn's pain, remembering her own. "And we lost Wayne Kresky. A boy named Dillard. That's enough blood for a very long time."

"As I said," Peggy reminded, "your experiences have put you in a unique position."

"I don't know," Amanda whispered.

"Well, that's as good a place to start as any."

"Start what?"

Peggy's eyes warmed. "The rest of your life, Amanda. It's yours for the taking."

14

THE ONCE-GLAMOROUS LOBBY of the DSI dormitory, located in a converted Anaheim hotel that gossip held served as the model for the Tower of Terror, was an unsettling mixture of brown tile, faded Oriental rugs, and sad furniture upholstered in a red fabric that looked like the material used for stage curtains. Art deco lights framed a six-foot-high black stone hearth that held illuminated, dreary potted plants. The often stale and dusty air didn't help with allergies; the most commonly heard sound throughout the building was sneezing.

The dorm's alleged connection to the scary Disney attraction did little to encourage the riding of the building's unusual "people movers." The elevators moved horizontally as well as vertically. Students typically took the stairs.

The ground-floor library boasted wall-to-wall shelves crammed with old leather-bound books, antique ceiling lights, and a few pieces of odd art grouped randomly on green marble-topped tables. Used for homework, research, and the occasional after-hours team meeting, the library offered anyone bold enough to visit an odd combination of cozy British great house and Disney's Haunted Mansion. Situated directly over the boiler room responsible for supplying hot water to all seventeen floors, the library played host to a variety of unusual, unexplained sounds that unsettled or frightened away its more timid occupants.

Amanda and Jess found their way there on a quiet Thursday night. They searched the stacks for a particular book and then, giving up, sat down in a pair of wingback chairs off in a corner.

At the other end of the small room, an extremely tall, thin boy sat alone, his face obscured by his abundance of wild black hair. Near him were two girls, both reading.

"So, is that him?" Jess whispered.

"I'm not positive, but yeah, he fits the description."

"Remember, don't ask me to do anything that will violate—"

"The code of conduct. Got it. You've said it like a hundred times." Having just sat down, Amanda rose and approached the two girls.

"Hi," she said brightly.

"Can we help you?" The girl who'd spoken was clearly of Scandinavian descent. She had the most gorgeous head of blond hair Amanda had ever seen, prettier even than Charlene's. Tons of it. Her high cheekbones, gleaming white teeth, and blue eyes made her look older than her friend, who looked more like a model for athletic wear.

"I'm looking for something called *Park History, 1957 through 1970*," Amanda said, holding out her hand to shake.

"Of course. Emily Fredrikson."

"Amanda Lockhart."

"History of Audio-Animatronics, Tuesday, second period, right?"

"Yeah."

"Thought I recognized you. You prefer cotton."

"I'm sorry?" Amanda said.

The girl sitting beside Emily laughed. "Em's a fabric geek. Second year, like me. And not fashion, fabric. If she dressed you, you'd find yourself in fibers made from snails' bacterial excretions."

"Unfair!" Emily said, laughing in spite of herself. "This is Tina, by the way."

Tina, a dark brunette with sharp blue eyes, had the complexion of a Scottish Highlander, with flushed red cheeks and fields of freckles.

"The first couple of months are tricky," Emily said, "but it gets better after that. Watch out for Tippy Kramer and her group. They think they're Walt's descendants and rightful heirs to his genius, something stupid like that."

"I appreciate the tip," Amanda said, nodding.

"Don't try too hard, and don't try to outsmart any of the 'teachers.'" Emily drew air quotes around the word. "All of them are Imagineers, which makes them Disney royalty. Most of them came up through the ranks the hard way, and I think they maybe see other talented people as threats."

"Oh," Amanda said.

"Forgive Emily her motherly instincts." Tina grimaced playfully. "She has only-child issues."

"Whatever, Tina," Emily said, all smiles once again. "So, what was the book?"

Amanda tried again. *Park History?*"

Jess joined them then, and the introductions started up again. Tina recognized Jess from Old Ways in the New World—An Introduction to Original Attractions, and they exchanged some small talk about the first class.

All the while, Emily studied Jess. "Double gauze top. Impressive. Aqua Washi?"

Caught off guard, Jess blushed. "I'm not sure."

"I'll explain later," Amanda said.

"About how big a fabric nerd I am," Emily said to Jess.

Emily caught Amanda's eye and pointed to the tall boy. "Your book's probably over there. If you can pry it away from Tim, you deserve it."

"But don't try to pry Tim," Tina said. "He's Em's."

"Utterly false! He thinks I'm his. There's a big difference."

"One of you's the telekinetic, right?" Tina asked. "I heard you could push."

Emily clucked her tongue disapprovingly. "Tina can be rude and nosy. Ignore her."

Tina chuckled. "I may be a little short on filters, but I never lie. I heard one of you was part of the Final Battle."

"Is that what it's being called?" Jess asked. "How dramatic."

"Neither of us is a big fan of labels," Amanda said.

But Tina couldn't help herself. "That doesn't answer my question."

"Give it a break, Tina," Emily said. "You two are obviously close. Friends from before?"

Amanda blinked at her tone. She sounded . . . threatened? But why?

"Since middle school, basically," Jess said. She didn't seem to notice Emily's suspicious air. "But under less than stellar conditions."

"How cool is that, though!" said Emily. "You guys are practically sisters."

"*Are* sisters. Both Lockhart. Both adopted." It was stretching the truth, though not by much.

"Unheard of," said Tina. "None of us knew each other before coming here. As in: none."

Now there was no missing it: an air of accusation and envy hung in the air between the pairs of girls.

Breaking the ice, Emily sweetly suggested that she and Amanda grab a Starbucks after their next class together. She sounded genuine.

"I'd love to hear how you two pulled off getting accepted together," Tina said, eyes still fixed on Jess.

Jess forced an unwilling smile. "Lucky, I guess."

Time to go. Amanda said good-bye and approached the boy, who wore headphones and a look of intense concentration as he read.

As the girls approached, he looked up and stared a little too long and too intimately at Amanda. He had brown eyes, a mat of unruly dark hair, and thick eyebrows.

"Yeah?" he said, slipping one ear clear of the headphones. His voice was adult and scratchy.

"Amanda. I'm new."

"Tim Walters. I'm not." He covered his ear back over.

"I was wondering if I could borrow *Park History*." She pointed to the book, which sat in a stack on the table in front of the boy.

He lifted the earphone, but Amanda wasn't about

to repeat herself. "I don't own it. That's why it's called a library."

"You're reading it."

"No. I'm reading this. It's just sitting there. That means it's yours if you want it."

"Seriously? You're good with that?"

"I didn't say that," Tim said. "I said it's yours if you want it."

"I'm not just going to take it," Amanda said stubbornly.

He flipped his arms as if to say, *Give me a break!*

"Hey, bonehead!" said Emily, kicking Tim's legs. The way they engaged, it was immediately apparent that they weren't strangers. Far from it. But they weren't close either, not exactly.

"Don't listen to this degenerate," Emily said. "Take the book. And if he gives you any trouble, let me know."

Tim stuck his tongue out at her.

"Very adult of you." Emily turned, making a point of her sultry sway as she went back to sit with Tina.

Tim pointed to the book in Amanda's arms. "It's not exactly Wikipedia, you know?"

"I'm trying to find out about the Imagineers' use of television in the parks. The history of it and stuff."

"No way!" Tim sat up sharply and ripped off the headphones, further tousling his unruly hair.

"Why? What?" Amanda said.

Beside her, Jess hid a smile, silently admiring Amanda's skill at working the boy. She and Amanda had researched Tim's field of study before coming to the library—but they weren't about to let him know that.

"Metaphorically speaking, alongside my name you'll see Tim-with-an-asterisk," Tim said.

"Why? Speaking metaphorically, of course."

"Because Imagineering communication technology is my specialty, my area of interest. My major, if we had majors."

"You're kidding me!" Amanda made her surprise sound genuine.

"What in particular interests you?" Tim asked.

"Probably better if I read up first. But your enthusiasm is noted."

"I'm not flirting."

"Okay."

"You think I'm flirting." He sounded crushed.

"I just think I need to do some reading before I talk to a person with an asterisk by his name."

"We live on the edge," Jess said, laughter obvious in her tone. Tim turned to her for the first time, jutting out his chin.

"You speak for each other, do you?"

"She takes the adjectives, I take the adverbs," Jess said.

"Feisty! I like that."

"No one asked," Jess said.

"Read all you want," Tim said, sitting back and kicking up his feet on the desk. "But I could save you a lot of time."

"How so?" Jess asked.

"Making things difficult if not impossible to reference has to be carefully planned." Tim shrugged. "I'm just saying. That may have gone on here."

"So you're a conspiracy theorist?" Jess said.

"I'm in lighting and sound, and the odd computer networking job."

"All computer networking is odd."

Amanda fought back a grin at Jess's quick comebacks.

Tim grinned, too. Nodded. Smiling was something that came naturally to him, it seemed. And he was far more handsome than Amanda had thought at first.

Catching herself, Amanda clutched the book tightly, and thanked Tim for it.

"Don't go too far," Tim said. "Because you'll be back."

Jess sighed, unimpressed, and followed Amanda back to their corner chairs. Tina called loudly after them, "Watch out for him, ladies. Killer smile, but he'd rather spend time with a circuit board than engage in active conversation."

"I have a love of learning!" Tim said, indignant.

In the book's index, Amanda found only a single reference for television: *Walt Disney's Wonderful World of Color*. There were four pages and they consisted almost entirely of photographs.

"He's right," she said. "Nothing here."

Tim was watching them. He seemed to be celebrating their failure.

"Little known fact," he called across the room. "*Set Design, 1950 through 1966* includes not only the addition of New Orleans Square, but the 1964 creation of Progressland for the General Electric Pavilion at the New York World's Fair."

"You're putting us to sleep over here," Tina called out.

"It's on the second shelf from the top, nearly all the way to your right," Tim said, directly to Jess.

Jess climbed the ladder, looked around, descended, and pushed the ladder to the end of the shelving unit. Absorbed in the photo spread, Amanda lost track of her. When she glanced curiously in the direction of Tim, his chair was empty. Only then did she hear the whispering voices behind her.

Tim stood one rung below Jess, well up the library ladder, arms around her on either side. He ran his long fingers along book spines, making a sound like a stick across a picket fence.

Watching them, Amanda missed Finn all the more.

"Got it," Tim said softly to Jess as he removed a book from the shelf. He helped her down, keeping one hand on the small of her back all the while.

Jess handed the book to Amanda.

Tim knelt down by her chair and spoke in a whisper. "The best stuff is supposed to be in a basement storage room."

"Best, as in?" Amanda whispered back.

"Senior theses, research papers, transcripts of nearly every lecture given at DSI. They publish less than ten percent of their institutional knowledge. The non-Disney-published books about the company are dismissed as uninformed or intentionally inflammatory. For the most part, that's true. But there are gems in nearly every one. Several mention the existence of DSI. Others describe an Imagineering research archive in the basement of the dorm building."

"You're making that up," Jess said.

"Have you ever met someone in lighting and sound who's this creative?" Tim's self-denigrating tone stopped the conversation. Jess sat back, miffed. Amanda filled the awkward silence by thanking Tim, who returned to his chair.

"Didn't look like you hated research all that much when you were on the ladder," Amanda said, moving from the book's index to its middle section, her eyes fixed on the page.

"I couldn't get the ladder to roll. Tim showed up to help. No biggie."

"Uh-huh," Amanda teased.

"Stop it!"

"Check this out." Amanda read quietly aloud. "'The concept for Carousel of Progress originated as part of the late nineteen fifties Edison Square expansion of Main Street USA. After the expansion fell through, the idea of a show celebrating the progress of technology was picked up and became 'Progressland' at the General Electric Pavilion at the 1964 New York World's Fair.'"

"Interesting."

"'Disney Imagineers Roger E. Broggie and Bob Gurr led the project. After the World's Fair ended, the attraction was moved to Disneyland, where it opened on July 2, 1967 under a new name, The Carousel of Progress. The attraction had the same sets and Audio-Animatronic performers as in the World's Fair, with only slight updates to the show's storyline.'"

"Huh. I still can't figure it out. Why would Finn and Philby ask about this?" Jess said.

Amanda passed Jess her phone. "Write this stuff down as I read?"

"Do I look like your secretary?" Jess complained. But she started thumb-typing the bullet points as Amanda continued.

"'Act One begins just before the turn of the century, with the advent of new-fangled inventions like the icebox and the "talking machine." Thanks to a new machine, it only takes Mother five hours to do the wash. Jane prepares to go out for a ride on an electric streetcar.

"'By Act Two, the nineteen twenties, the house is outfitted in electric lights and indoor plumbing, making ironing easier on Mother, and helping Cousin Orville keep cool in the bathtub.

"'Act Three, the Roaring Forties, has Grandma wearing a hearing aid while Mother uses her electric mixer to mix paint. Jane is keeping in shape with an electric machine while she ties up the house phone.

"'Act Four depicts the future, with electric appliances that make the 1967 Christmas dinner a breeze. Jet travel provides a means for Grandma and Grandpa to visit, while a new color TV offers entertainment.'

"Did you get that?" Amanda said, pausing. "TV. It's mentioned right there."

"Did I get it all? No. Enough? Yes. And note to Amanda: we should be doing our real homework."

"Okay, go. And, thank you! I can do this by myself." Amanda reached out to take back her phone.

"No, I'll stick around and help," Jess said begrudgingly.

"And that has nothing to do with Tim," Amanda whispered.

Jess kicked her.

Amanda read on, this time taking notes herself.

"'On September 9, 1973, the show closed for a cross-country move, opening in Walt Disney World on January 15, 1975. The theaters now rotated counterclockwise rather than clockwise. Changes included: no post show, an updated fourth act, and a new theme song called "The Best Time of Your Life."'"

One of many footnotes read: "COP was updated in 1985, and again in 1993."

"Good evening, all!" The deeply sonorous voice belonged to a tall man with silver hair and matching eyebrows, dressed in the ubiquitous khaki pants and School of Imagineering polo that marked DSI instructors. He stood in the library's lobby door beside a matronly woman with a trim figure, long neck, and prominent nose.

"I am Tobias Langford. You may call me Toby. In my company is Ms. Bernice Crenshaw—"

"Bernie!" the woman called out.

Those in the library, including Tim, Tina, Emily, Amanda, and Jess, all looked up.

"First years, remind us of your names, please?" Ms. Bernie Crenshaw said.

Amanda and Jess turned out to be the only two first years present. Tobias Langford took down their names in a flip-cover spiral notebook.

"Bernie, have they done something wrong?" Emily asked.

"Yeah, are they in trouble?" Tina said, a little too enthusiastically.

"On the contrary," Langford said. "We are duly impressed by any first years who instigate the use of our facilities' expanded offerings. Excellent! The use of the library suggests . . . overachievers."

"We'll just have a quick look at the books you're reading, if you don't mind." Crenshaw's voice cut as sharp as a crow's cry.

Jess shot Amanda a suspicious glance.

Amanda caught Tim's eyes moving between her and, more specifically, the two books on the table in front of her.

Also seeing Tim, Jess reacted before Amanda, touching the bottom book: *Park History*. Tim gently rocked his head side to side. *Not that one.*

Jess tapped the top book, *Set Design 1950–1966*.

Almost imperceptibly, Tim nodded.

Quickly, Jess slipped *Set Design* off the table and stashed it behind her. But the book's location made her sit stiffly in the chair, so she slid it beneath the seat cushion and wiggled down onto it like a hen onto an egg.

She looked up and saw the two faculty members standing close by. Langford smelled of leathery cologne. He was taller up close.

"Tobias Langford," he repeated, offering his hand to both girls. They shook. "Dean of Technology and Innovation."

"You must know Tim, then," Jess said.

"Indeed." Langford spun to look at Walters.

"You may call him Toby, and me, Bernie," the woman said. "As you've no doubt heard, all faculty prefer to be addressed by their first names."

"Yes, ma'am," Jess said, out of habit.

"What have we here?" Tobias Langford asked, picking up the park history book from the table.

"*Park History*, for our History of Audio-Animatronics course," Amanda said, offering the explanation a little too quickly and enthusiastically. Nervously.

"Yes," he said, towering above her. His expression held a doubtful, penetrating inquiry that caught Amanda by surprise. "Nineteen sixty-three."

"Excuse me?"

"The first use of the term. Audio-Animatronics were introduced in the Tiki Room, but had been in development for several years prior."

"Ooookay." The drawled word escaped Amanda's lips before she could stop herself.

"You don't ever want to leave a book open upside down like this," Bernie Crenshaw said, reaching down. "It can damage the binding. Please use a—" She stopped.

She'd opened the book to the page Amanda had been reading.

Without speaking, she passed the book to Tobias. He read deliberately, and then examined the placement of the library ladder, the rows of books, and the prominent gap on the upper shelf. Still in silence, he shifted his burning inquisitive gaze to Amanda.

Bernie spoke. "We are pleased to see you taking advantage of the resources available here in Asher House." Asher House was the proper name for the Tower. "How has your experience been so far?"

"Great," Amanda said.

"Terrific," Jess added. "I am so honored to be here, to have this opportunity."

"We expect great things from both of you," Toby said. "From all our students." He pivoted. "Don't we,

Tim?" It was a pointed remark, the subtleties of which Amanda couldn't quite discern.

Tim nodded sheepishly. "Of course."

"We will be watching you all . . . enthusiastically." He delivered this while looking into Amanda's eyes with an intensity she wanted to shy away from—and finally did.

"It's going to be a great year," Bernie said.

"Enjoy your . . . reading." Toby made a point of staring at the high shelf, and at the vacant slot left by the book that currently lay beneath Jess's seat cushion.

"Always," Amanda said. It came out sounding like a confession.

LAKE BUENA VISTA, FLORIDA

Walt Disney World

⋇The wise camel is not swayed by desert mirages; instead, it trudges on, in search for true water.*

---

*Abandoned_Wishes

15

Invited by Rich Fleming, Disney World's Entertainment Operations Manager, to view Illumi-Nations as a group from the VIP dock near Epcot's Mexico pavilion, the Keepers—minus Charlene, who'd remained in Hollywood for work—assembled at eight forty-five p.m. by the rope that blocked entry to the VIP area.

On all sides, the mob of park guests pressed close to the railings, each striving to get the best view of the spectacular. Some autograph seekers caught up to the Keepers, mostly kids. A few diehard Disney adults thanked them for "preserving the dream," "saving the parks," "protecting us all."

Welcomed, and let through the barrier, the Keepers walked out onto the dock and formed a huddle ahead of the show's start, which featured a combination of fire, water, lasers, fireworks, and music.

Unnoticed in the melee, Finn showed them the fountain pen drawn on his forearm. Philby pointed out that Finn was right-handed and could never have drawn the pen himself.

"Which implies that you guys don't trust me," Finn said. "That you actually think I might do that. Wonderful feeling, by the way."

"So what happened, exactly?" Maybeck asked, ignoring him.

Finn and Philby exchanged a look. Slowly, Philby said, "His memory was wiped."

"That's convenient," Maybeck said. He spoke under his breath, but loud enough that everyone could hear.

"Shut up!" Willa came to Finn's defense, surprising him. "Let's listen. Okay?"

"Of primary importance," Philby said, "is the message itself: the pen. Obviously, we aren't the only ones worried that without it being in One Man's Dream, we never save the park."

"Do you know how stupid that sounds?" Maybeck said.

"'It's about time,'" Philby said. "Remember Wayne's words."

"Time for what?" Maybeck said.

"Well, that's the thing. We thought he meant his watch, right? And he did. We found a bunch of clues on it. But you know how Wayne was. With him, there were levels to everything. So we follow the clues. I cross over Finn. Finn ends up returning with a pen drawn on his arm—despite never leaving King Arthur Carrousel.

So who drew it, and why doesn't Finn remember?"

"And who cares?" Maybeck said sternly. "We're moving on, right?"

Willa nodded. But only Willa.

"Wayne led us to the music box. The music box led to his message. His message led to Finn's crossing over," Philby said, recounting the events like a trial attorney. "This was something planned carefully. Elaborately. Now the pen appears on Finn's arm. Finn loses his memory. And that's the point when we move on, Terry? Does that feel like closure to you? If it does, fine. Move on. No one's going to stop you or Willa or Charlene. But I can't. Not yet."

Finn kept his head down, trying to hide his wonder. To hear Philby—of all people, Philby!—defend him! He marveled at the turnaround. For years the two had been rivals, both eager to lead the Kingdom Keepers. Now, they were speaking, thinking, as one.

"That sounds so strange coming from you," Willa said, verbalizing what Finn was thinking.

"So where are you going with this?" Maybeck asked.

"More tests are needed." From attorney to doctor in less than a minute. Classic Professor Philby. "More help."

"Oh, man. Here we go," Maybeck moaned.

"What kind of tests?" Willa asked.

"There's an easy way, and a hard way," Philby said.

"There's a surprise," Maybeck said. "For once, just once, can we try the easy way?"

"Not without Joe's help," Philby said, checking his watch. He tapped his phone and initiated a video call. The name *Joe Garlington* appeared across his screen.

As the phone started to ring, Philby said, "Let me do the talking."

16

THE MISSION: SPACE PAVILION was virtually empty. With nearly the entire guest population distracted by the greatest nighttime outdoor entertainment show in the United States, the four Keepers entered and were met by a Cast Member, who'd been sent by Joe.

"Sorry for all the cloak-and-dagger," the young woman said, addressing Philby. "But as Joe may have explained, given the rushed nature of your request, this was the only location in which we could show you the video in complete privacy."

"We understand."

She led the way down the ride's empty exit line.

"As it happens, our simulators accommodate four. They have video and sound. The video you requested will be uploaded directly from Disney Studios. Only you four will see it. Once we close you in, you'll have complete privacy."

"So we don't actually have to take the ride?" Maybeck asked hopefully.

"I'm afraid you do. The videos run when the attraction is moving. There just isn't time to change that synchronization. You will be the only ones riding the attraction. The other simulators will all be empty. The line is light at the moment. It shouldn't be a problem."

They reached a large, circular room rimmed with a dozen simulators. At the sight, Maybeck went green, and instinctively put a hand to his stomach.

"I get sick on this ride," he muttered.

"Yes, well, you're not alone there," the young woman said, smiling.

"Philby?"

"Get in."

* * *

The attraction was designed to simulate blasting off in a rocket, slingshotting around the moon, and encountering a meteor field. Because of this, the sound track included messages from Ground Control to the spacecraft, and the simulator pod moved in a high-speed circular motion while also banking left and right. Normally, the screen would have shown flight images, including deep space, the moon, and Mars. The jerking, rocking movement of the pod typically coordinated with the story in the video.

But for the Keepers, the view was of Finn, alone, in night vision green and black, traveling around in circles on King Arthur Carrousel. It was the security video Philby had requested from Joe. The Keepers watched as Finn moved from horse to horse. The attraction came to a stop. Finn got off. The tape jumped ahead; Finn climbed onto Jingles.

The video was shot at a distance by a stationary camera well hidden from park guests. The carousel looked tiny; Finn was a little over an inch tall.

Over the sound track that accompanied the roller-coaster movements of the simulator pod—all four kids were glad they'd eaten dinner several hours earlier—Finn shouted, "This . . . is . . . so . . . weird!"

"Think how we feel!" Maybeck called back.

With Finn's hologram on Jingles, there was a brief technical problem with the tape. It looked as if a hair or piece of lint had attached itself right to Finn's horse.

And then . . .

Finn disappeared.

Philby noted the passage of time and did some math—counting fifteen minutes and thirty-four seconds—edited from the tape. For a second time, a hair caught on the camera, and then Finn reappeared, in stark black and green instead of green and black. A fraction of a second later, he flipped back.

Maybeck nearly puked, but burped instead. By this point, he was as green as night vision Finn.

When the ride finally stopped and the door opened, a man stood just off to the side.

"Brad?" Finn said, his face lighting up. This was the Imagineer who had first modeled the young Finn, Willa, Charlene, Maybeck, and Philby, using a green screen sound studio to create their DHIs.

"In the flesh," he said. "This way, please."

Brad led them upstairs to an oddly shaped VIP lounge. The space held four lounge chairs and a pair of large beanbags, as well as a bizarre electric-aquamarine coffee table that looked more like a miniature trampoline. A flat-panel television was mounted high on the wall, opposite the large floor-to-ceiling windows.

"What's up?" Finn said, once Brad had asked them to sit down. The door was securely shut, making the whole meeting all the more mysterious.

"You should have told us." Though Finn had spoken, Brad directed his words at Philby.

"I know."

"We made those edits tonight. That's why they were rough."

"I thought that was the case," Philby said.

"What's the deal?" Maybeck asked.

"Do you want to tell them?" Brad asked Philby, catching him off guard.

"Um."

Brad asked Finn what he remembered about the carousel ride. Finn checked quickly with Philby, who dipped his chin in the barest possible nod.

"Nothing. Not a thing. Zero. Zilch."

Brad's expression froze. He grunted. "Okay, then. I guess we're done here. Thanks. And sorry for the bother."

"I don't think so," Philby said, winning Brad's full attention.

"I gave you your chance," Brad said.

"The lint on the lens." Philby met him glare for glare.

"What about it?"

Maybeck had risen to his feet; Philby waved him back down onto his beanbag. Slouching and extending his long legs, Maybeck said, "Just in case anyone cares, there's no way that was edited tonight."

"Exactly!" Philby said.

"Exactly what?" Brad asked.

Willa sat up taller. "Can someone speak English here?"

It was Philby who answered her. "I'm guessing the Imagineers, or maybe the Cryptos, have seen this 'lint' before." He drew air quotes. "It wasn't something on the lens."

Maybeck jumped in. "Which would explain why the

dead time was edited out of the video. Why it's only the important moments."

Philby: "How many times?"

Brad: "Seven."

Philby: "Which attractions? No, no! Don't tell me! Storybook Land, Snow White, Peter Pan's Flight, Mr. Toad's Wild Ride, Mad Tea Party—"

Willa: "—Jungle Cruise and King Arthur Carrousel."

Brad nodded slowly. "Well, well. Impressive, you two."

Maybeck shook his head. "What about Finn and me? Spread the praise around!"

Finn barely seemed to hear. He was bent forward in his chair, fingers steepled together in front of his face. "No Autopia?"

Philby beamed at him. "Very good!"

"No," Brad said. "That attraction has no connection to a former work."

Frustration overwhelmed Maybeck. "Hello!? What's going on?"

Finn turned to him, his back straightening, excitement dawning on his face. "Willa and Philby listed the attractions on opening day in Disneyland that are told as stories."

Philby said, "The Imagineers, maybe the guests, have seen these anomalies, these odd shimmers—this lint—on the security cameras, before. Am I right?"

"You are," said Brad. "We've shut down attractions, sometimes for a few hours, sometimes for weeks, trying to analyze what's taking place."

"And you came to a conclusion, didn't you?" Philby said. He sounded impossibly certain. "Or in Imagineer-speak, a theory."

Brad pursed his lips. "I think we're done here."

"No, we are not," Finn said. "You are not going anywhere until you tell us what the heck is going on."

"It's about time," Philby said. "That is, time is what it's about. Time is the subject. Time is what Wayne wanted us to focus on, to understand. To explore."

"Don't get ahead of yourselves," Brad said, frowning.

"Hard to get ahead when we're so far behind," Maybeck said. "What is this lint?"

"Cracks. Seams," Philby said, staring straight at Brad. The Imagineer looked terrified by the direction the conversation had taken. "And what did your team find? Data surges, occurring just prior to each appearance of the lint. And they found that Wayne Kresky was never seen in public during those same periods."

Brad's face was ashen. Sweat beaded on his forehead. "We shouldn't be having this discussion."

"Data surges. Holograms," Willa said. "Oh my

God. Was Wayne self-projecting his DHI? That is seriously risky."

"What he was attempting was far more risky than self-projection," Philby said.

Maybeck spoke quickly. "Name one thing more dangerous than not having someone to help you if the Return fails. That's Sleeping Beauty Syndrome, but with no one knowing you need help. It's suicide."

"Why would he risk that?" Finn said, shaking his head. "Why take that kind of chance?"

Willa's voice was so soft that everyone in the room had to strain forward to hear. "Because that's the risk every pioneer takes." She was looking at Philby the way Philby was looking at Brad. It seemed as if no one in the room was breathing.

Outside, the fireworks from IllumiNations exploded loudly and rapidly in the grand finale. Bright light and shadows mixed in the VIP lounge, filling the room until the space seemed to have no floor, no ceiling. Finn felt as if he were falling.

"Pioneer?" Maybeck choked out. "Like what kind of pioneer?"

Brad wouldn't answer, so Philby did.

"The time travel kind."

ANAHEIM, CALIFORNIA

Disney School of Imagineering

ЖКThe danger of falling could destroy you,
But the price of safety might not be worth it.*

---

*President_Escher

17

"If you stand on your tiptoes, your hair's going to hit the lights," Amanda said, looking up at the elevator car's cciling.

"You're obsessed with my height. I'm tall. Great. There's not that much I can do about it."

"Believe me, I'm not obsessed with anything about you. Don't fool yourself."

The elevator's doors closed, but the car did not move.

"You need to answer something for me," Tim said, leaning back against the wall and casually crossing his arms. "Why the interest in early television in the park? You don't strike me as a radio technology freak."

"What's it to you?" Amanda said, exasperated. "Why are you doing this, anyway? Helping me?"

"Helping you and Jessica," he corrected.

"That's hardly an answer. You've been here over a year now. You could have done this research anytime. Why now?"

"Stand back, and hold on tight," Tim instructed, leaning forward and giving her a sly grin.

"I'm perfectly fine, thank you."

He pushed and held three buttons on the panel. The elevator car did not move up or down. Instead, with a heaving jerk, it jumped violently to the right. Amanda fell to the floor. Tim did not.

Groaning, Amanda pulled herself to her knees.

"I'd stay down there, if I were you," Tim said.

The elevator lurched backward. It jerked to a second stop. The car fell away, dropping as if its cable had been cut.

Amanda bit her lips to keep from screaming.

The car bounced. The doors opened, revealing a dark basement.

"To be continued . . ." Tim whispered, dragging her by the hand out of the car and across a dark, open space into a tangle of wide pipes. Before she could speak, he pressed his hand over her mouth. "I probably should have mentioned that Dirk the Jerk lives down here. The janitor. Don't worry he's ancient."

As if in response, there came the sound of shoes scraping the floor. A human shadow approached, stretched thin and ghostly on the floor's surface. It had a pinched head, sloping shoulders, a long narrow body, and pencil legs fifteen feet long. The shadow soon joined at the feet with a pair of paint-splattered brown leather boots. The work pants that fell over the boots were faded gray from years of laundering.

Dirk, the man wearing the pants, was unshaven, greasy-haired, and bony. His forehead jutted out like the bill of a hat, all but hiding a pair of small eyes, a beak of a nose. He walked stiffly, like his joints had frozen, swinging his arms like canoe paddles.

Tim tugged Amanda down behind the three-foot-diameter pipe. She couldn't see, only imagine, the maintenance man inspecting the elevator. He moved closer to Tim and Amanda and stopped, sniffing the air. Amanda had shampooed that morning. Strawberry peach.

Beads of sweat left silver lines down Tim's face. His full lips had gone pale. Amanda gave him a thumbs-up. Tim didn't look convinced.

Then the scratching of the boots against the concrete retreated. Several minutes passed.

Tim exhaled audibly. "That was close."

"I could tell you about close," Amanda said softly, "but I'll save that for another time. Wherever we're going, let's make it fast. I'm beginning to think Jess was the smart one."

"I have a theory, based on the hotel electric schematics."

"Wait." Amanda paused, looked at him incredulously. "You don't know where we're going?"

"Has to be in the far corner of the basement," Tim said doggedly. "There's a separate air-conditioning system and dehumidifier. It was all retrofitted. That's where we start."

"When you say far, how far is the 'far corner'?"

"Well, Amanda, it's a big hotel."

"Hardly reassuring. What's between here and there?"

"Probably nothing."

"Probably?" She sat back, wiped cobwebs from her face.

"I'm not a regular visitor! Some storage, maybe. The hotel had a full kitchen and laundry back in the day. If they're still here, they'd be centrally located."

"I need to know: why do you care about the Imagineering archives so much?"

"We can talk about this later," Tim said, and turned away, crouching to avoid banging his head as he ducked and maneuvered through the pipes. Amanda had no choice but to follow.

"I think we should talk about this now," she said, slightly louder.

Tim shushed her. For a tall kid, he was incredibly limber and agile. She worked to keep up.

An aisle appeared to the right. A bare concrete floor; high metal shelving on both sides, all of it crowded with open plastic crates and boxes. A thick black stripe ran straight down the aisle's center.

Tim pointed out a concrete block structure, eight feet square, and spoke in a whisper. "Far side of the lobby. That's the support for the fireplace."

"Fascinating."

"I'm just saying."

Amanda rolled her eyes, but kept quiet. They were finding a rhythm, moving like police sneaking up on a suspect.

"Interesting," Tim said, looking up overhead. "I think there might have been dumbwaiters here. What's now the cafeteria used to be the hotel dining room, so that would make sense."

They reached a door. Tim tried it. Locked. Soon, another door. The handle turned. The door opened, and they stepped inside. Amanda eased the door shut, and Tim activated his phone's flashlight function, shining a wide swath of light into a huge room filled with cobwebs, old machinery, dangling wires, long tables, and carts with rotting scabbed canvas. Part horror movie, part History Channel, the hotel's former laundry room was a museum of antique washing machines, industrial mangles, rods, and racks. Regularly spaced wooden tables for folding and sorting the laundry turned it into an obstacle course. It looked as if people had abandoned it quickly. A long time ago.

Shuddering, Amanda unwound a wire hanger and used it to dislodge the spiderwebs clotting their path.

"Do you see all the rat droppings?" she asked.

"Noted."

Together, but with Amanda leading, they crept through the cavernous room. The only sound was their footsteps, and a quiet rustle of the hanger in the webs.

"Do you believe in ghosts?" Tim asked.

"Is that a trick question?" Amanda said. "I happen to love the Haunted Mansion. I still get shivers when I'm in there."

"That's different." Tim cast his eyes left and right, then shuddered. "This looks like everyone just walked away from what they were doing and never came back. I find that disturbing."

"You're not alone in that," Amanda said wryly. "But what would cause something like this? An earthquake? A fire?"

Tim stopped abruptly. "Wait a second! The story behind the Tower of Terror: five people disappear from an elevator during a horrific lightning strike. Think about it. Lightning. Electricity."

"Is that what you're after? The truth about what happened to this hotel?"

"Come on, Amanda. Do you understand the

significance to Disney history? If the inspiration for the ride is this hotel and not the Hollywood Tower hotel, then this building may well be haunted!" Tim's eyes were wide and frantic in the pale light of his cell phone.

"If everybody in the hotel had been wiped out in a lightning strike, don't you think we'd know about it?" Amanda swatted at more cobwebs, resumed her forward movement.

"Not if it was part of a bigger disaster. I'm sorry to say the people in this hotel would have been just a statistic. And if there *were* stories written about it, where would those newspaper articles reside?"

They'd reached a door clear across the room on the far wall. Tim held the doorknob but waited to turn it.

"Answer the question," he said.

"Okay. I'd hide them in an archive. A secret archive. And I'd hire someone to live in the basement and keep an eye on all those secrets." Amanda paused. "Fine. I get it now. But . . . why bring me?"

"You think I was going to come down here alone? I may be dumb, but I'm not stupid."

Amanda answered with a frank, grim expression. "There's something wrong here. I'll give you that much." Chills racked her body, shooting along her limbs. "I think maybe I've seen enough."

"You realize how close you are to the history of television and video technology in the parks? Look, all basements are weird. This one in particular. But did I feel a wave of cold or fingers around my neck? No, I did not. Not even close. I just freaked myself out." Tim smiled ruefully. "And I freaked you out, too. Hey, when I was a kid, my brother used to tie me up and leave me in the basement. We had a big house, very old, and the basement was cold and smelled bad. I still have nightmares. But I fight past it. You have to ask yourself: what are you trying to find, Amanda? And why? Don't try the word 'curiosity.' I'm not buying."

"Fine," Amanda said tartly, "because I'm not selling."

"Sure you are. You've been selling since we met. You just happened to want my book? Just happened to need help in my area of interest? Do you want to try again? Start all over?"

"Think what you want," Amanda said.

"That's not an answer. You're avoiding the question."

"You first."

They locked eyes in the dark. After a moment, Tim shrugged and said, "There are some interesting historical overlaps I need verified. Technical observations. If you look closely, really closely, at the history of

Imagineering, you find uncanny connections between big technological jumps in video transmission—think, television—radio/wireless devices, and Disney. There are all these rumors. I'd love to confirm or debunk them."

"See?" Amanda said. "That wasn't so hard! Telling the truth is a lot easier than it sounds."

"Easier for me than you, apparently," Tim said, fighting a grin. He motioned forward, but Amanda slipped behind him, allowing him to lead the way down yet another aisle framed by towering shelves. These held paint cans, replacement furniture, plumbing parts, light fixtures, toilets. It looked like a hardware superstore.

The faintest sound startled them both. A creak. A drip of water. Gurgling pipes. The grind of distant machinery, a continuous whine from the overhead tube lights.

Tim's obvious anxiety was a relief to Amanda. She whispered, "Have you ever noticed that *scared* and *sacred* are basically the same word?"

In spite of himself, Tim almost laughed. "Never."

A sound like a whirring kitchen mixer rose up to overpower all others.

"What is that?" Amanda hissed.

Ahead of her, Tim had reached an intersection of aisles; his attention was fully absorbed by the black paint stripe at their feet, which split left, right, and continued straight.

"It's such ancient technology," he breathed, "I didn't recognize what it was!"

She wasn't going to say anything. He resembled a bloodhound on the scent and she didn't want to get bit. Tim checked in both directions, brushing his hair out of his eyes.

"I can't see it yet, but I hear it."

"It? Who? What?" Amanda let slip, and instantly chastised herself. "Forget I asked! I didn't mean to say any—"

"Shut up!" he snapped, and went back to listening intently, moving his head to hear. "Okay. Here's what we're going to do." He backed up, knelt, and waved her down alongside. "We're going to belly-crawl over there." He pointed across the intersection to the same aisle they were now in. "As we do, you're going to look right. I'll look left. We keep low and we keep moving no matter what. Got it?"

"No, I don't 'got it'! Why? What's out there?"

"The three-nineties have slow focus!" Tim said. "Once we're across—"

"Wait! What's a three-ninety?"

"Once across, we'll hide until he passes. After that, we should be okay."

"He? Dirk?"

"I wish!" Tim said. "Ready?"

"No, I'm not—"

But Tim dropped to his stomach and crawled out into the intersection of aisles. Amanda joined him, mimicking his moves.

At first she thought what she saw was some sort of industrial vacuum or cleaner. But it wasn't that at all.

A twelve-inch diameter metallic cylinder rose from its moving base to an inverted triangle of metal at the top. Perched on the triangle was a silver ball with three glass lenses aimed out. A tri-clops robot. Fat, black rubber hoses created shoulders and elbows. On one arm a claw, and the other four fingers. The head spun like an owl's.

Shaking with fear, Amanda crawled across the intersection and crouched by Tim.

"It's a robot!" she hissed.

"A STAN three-ninety. Way ahead of its time when the Imagineers introduced it. Ancient technology now; prehistoric, really." He urged her onto the lowest shelf behind them and climbed up alongside of her.

"Put your back against this pallet," he said.

"But . . . I mean . . . a robot!"

"Yeah. Amazing it still runs. It tracks along the magnetic strip painted on the floor. It was initially used in inventory robotics; the Imagineers wrote about three-nineties someday replacing librarians. This goes to my earlier point: the Imagineers aren't credited with half of what they apparently invented. I want to fix that."

Tim seemed to be talking to himself. "A three-ninety doesn't see well below eighteen inches," he muttered. "If we stay low on the shelf, we should be okay."

"Should be?"

"The question is," Tim said, staring into the space before them, "who revived a three-ninety, and why? Dirk?"

"Is it dangerous?" Amanda asked. To her surprise, Tim answered.

"Could be, if it's been modified. Wasn't designed that way. It can probably record video. Possibly broadcast live sound. Dirk's been busy, it seems."

"All this leaves us where, exactly?"

"Stuck," Tim said. "I suggest we don't exactly test it. If we move, it's going to see us. If it sees us and it's broadcasting, we're seen by whoever's monitoring it. Once it gets out of here, we can head over to the next aisle and keep going."

"This does not sound good," Amanda said.

"Look at it this way: We must have presented some kind of threat if a three-ninety was dispatched to patrol the area. Right? This is a very good sign!"

"It seems more like we should turn around. Go back."

"Are you kidding? We just got here."

"The farther we go, the deeper we're in," Amanda said.

"I know! Fun, isn't it?"

18

THE STAN 390 GROUND ITS WAY along the magnetic stripe, turning down the aisle that harbored Tim and Amanda. As it groaned past, the two held their breaths reflexively, and then rolled off the shelf into the next aisle. The shelving in this row held bare mattresses and pillows wrapped in plastic, dozens of dressers, and hundreds of desk lamps.

Once they escaped, they moved carefully, keeping track of the robot through gaps in the contents on the shelves. They checked in all directions, stopping randomly to listen.

A minute later, the sounds changed. A steady groan behind them. Another ahead and well to their right.

Tim held up two fingers. Two 390s closing in. Possibly a third the next aisle over. Tim and Amanda were being squeezed.

Quietly, his face resolute, Tim tore open a packet of cloth napkins. He and Amanda tied them around their faces like bandits. Then they climbed up on another shelf and lay down flat. A different sound, like a garbage truck picking up a trash can, filled the air. Tim rose on his arms as if he were doing a push-up. A claw appeared and stabbed out at his shoulder. There was a buzz; the smell of ozone hung in the air, and Tim shook, electrified. Stunned.

Trying to keep her breathing level steady to reduce her growing panic, Amanda dragged him out of reach of the probe. The 390 readjusted its claw. Amanda dragged a box toward her, hoping to use it as a shield. But the packaging was old. The cardboard crumbled like ash, revealing a framed mirror.

Tim moaned, coming awake.

Amanda shifted the mirror, tilting it so the 390's lens would aim at its surface. Behind her, Tim came up on an elbow.

The 390 made a spinning sound, its optics—or the man running them—seemingly confused.

But the respite was short-lived. The support beneath her shook and rattled. The 390 was pulling the shelving apart, trying to dislodge its contents. Including Tim and Amanda.

"What the . . . ?" Tim slurred, as he and Amanda slid to the edge.

Amanda saw no other choice. She *pushed* the 390. It fell over. Again.

Sounds of twisting metal filled the room like a soda

can crushing under a shoe. An array of sparks was followed by a puff of smoke.

"Can you move?" Amanda asked.

"Did you do that?" Tim croaked.

"Follow me," she said.

"How did you do that?"

"Shut up and follow me!"

Amanda slipped over the side of the shelf and climbed down, her face pinched with worry.

19

HAVING LED A RECOVERING TIM back to the laundry room, Amanda crossed to the far door, hoping to reach the elevators. A loud buzz on the other side of the door spurred her into action. A 390.

"No good! Help me!" she called.

She and Tim slid a heavy piece of machinery forward to block the door.

"The other door!" A 390 could be heard there as well. Moving fast, she and Tim shut the door and blocked it with a cabinet.

"Trapped," Tim gasped.

The doors banged and shook; the doorjambs cracked and gave way. As both doors pushed open an inch or two, Tim uttered an expletive Amanda would rather not have heard.

"Steady!" Using her phone as a flashlight, Amanda surveyed the room. The industrial clothes dryers might be large enough to hide in, but once in, there was no way out. Towering coiled springs arced over the ironing tables, meant to hold the wire away from the hot iron.

Pulling himself together, Tim spotted two identical

wood-slatted cabinets. "Dumbwaiters!" He pushed the button to the side of the door. Nothing.

"No power!" Tim complained loudly.

"What did you say?" Her brain had confused the word "power" with "powder." *No powder!*

She spotted a group of metal garbage cans alongside the laundry machines. Inside was white, powdery detergent.

The force on both doors continued. The barriers Tim and Amanda had put in place were slipping and giving way, the doors slowly opening.

Tim wandered across the room, his eyes trained onto the ceiling. He banged into a folding table.

"Hey, snap out it!" she called.

"Shut it! I'm working, princess."

"I need help over here."

No response. Realizing Tim was useless, Amanda dragged the first can of detergent to the closest door and dumped its contents onto the floor. Soap flakes, like a pile of sand. She dragged another toward the opposite door.

"A little help!" she called. The cans were heavy; she was out of breath. "Please!"

"Not now, princess."

"Do . . . not . . . call me that!" Amanda managed to dump the second can in front of the opening door.

"Got it!" Tim called out.

Both doors continued to move. They'd be open in a matter of seconds.

"Masks up!" Amanda hollered, pulling her own napkin covering back into place.

Tim stood in front of an electrical panel. His eyes were vacant and bright, fixed on a spot in the distance.

"Electricity," Amanda said, wonder in her tone.

"That's the idea! For the dumbwaiters!" he called back, tripping one circuit breaker after another. Most did nothing—and then the overhead lights flashed on.

To Amanda's left, the 390's electronic claw maneuvered inside and—amazingly!—swept the piece of heavy machinery aside as if it were an empty cardboard box. The door gave way.

Amanda ran to the washing machines. She worked furiously to unscrew the hoses but couldn't overcome the decades of rust. Involuntarily, she formed a fist and pounded the machine out of sheer frustration.

The washing machine slid five feet along the floor.

Amanda gasped as the hose she'd been battling tore off from the back of the washer. She'd *pushed* without thinking about it. Without focusing. With her fist! A first! She seized the hose and cranked a stubborn faucet. The hose burped, jumped, coughed, and spit. Brown water shot from it like a fire hose.

At the same instant, a 390 grumbled through the nearest door and rolled forward into the pile of laundry detergent that covered its magnetic floor stripe. Its underlying wheels and rollers crunched; the robot sprayed dry detergent behind it like a dog digging a hole.

Amanda aimed the water stream into a long, high rainbow arc. It fell short. She raised the hose higher. The detergent roiled into suds as the stream splashed at the base of the robot. Sparks exploded, smoke coiled. The robot belched a nasty gray haze and went silent. Dead.

"YES!" Tim cheered.

Amanda swung the hose to her right. The other 390 had also faltered in the detergent. It tipped over and smashed to the concrete. She doused it, rendering it a smoking heap of short-circuited metal.

"Over here!" Tim held a dumbwaiter open. "You first," he said, motioning her inside the small box—an elevator for laundry baskets.

"Who's there?" a old man's voice called into the space.

Dirk, Amanda thought angrily. Dirk the Jerk.

"I'll take the other one," Tim whispered. "Hurry!" He pushed her lightly, urging her in.

"But the button's on the outsi—"

Tim stuffed her inside, slid the wood-slatted barrier down, and pushed the button.

Nothing happened. He cursed and slapped the dumbwaiter's call button once, then again.

The small cage shook and groaned. For Amanda, everything went dark.

20

"STOP!" DIRK. His voice was furious and loud.

Tim wedged himself into the remaining dumbwaiter. As Amanda had pointed out, one couldn't trip the call button from inside because the gate had to be lowered first.

He pulled the gate shut, kicked hard, and broke one of the slats. He reached through and punched the button. The dumbwaiter ascended. But Tim's wrist was stuck, caught between the slats. As the dumbwaiter dragged upward, his hand would be cut off.

Dirk pushed through the laundry room door.

Tim yanked his hand free just before it would have been severed. The dumbwaiter's interior went dark. From where Dirk stood, he saw only the last few inches of an ascending dumbwaiter and, through its gate, a pair of blue Converse All Stars.

The image of the shoes lodged firmly in his mind as he looked down and cried out, bemoaning the destruction of his beloved 390s.

21

"So, HOW WAS IT? You look sweaty," Jess told Amanda as she entered their dorm room.

Amanda collapsed onto the bed beneath her lavishly decorated wall. Her hair was plastered to her forehead, and her cheeks were deeply flushed.

"Okay, I guess."

"Tell me."

"Nothing special. Just a big basement."

"You smell like laundry soap, and your shoes are wet. So are your pants. You're beet red, too, and your hair's a mess."

"We found the laundry room. We were a little . . . active. It's not much, believe me."

"I want to believe you," Jess said.

"What's that supposed to mean?"

"It means you're not telling me something and you don't sound like yourself."

"Look, if I tell you, Jess, and anyone asks you about what happened down there, you'll have to lie. And you don't want to be part of this. Right?"

"So what, you're protecting me now?"

"I'm trying to, yes."

"If you're protecting me, something bad happened."

Amanda said nothing.

"What about the archives?"

Nothing.

"So you're not going to tell me anything? This is me, Mandy!"

Nothing.

"You're mad at me for not going." Jess sounded sick. She sat back blindly, dropping down onto the bed. "We do everything together, but I didn't do this, and you're mad."

"That's not true."

"You pushed! Oh my gosh, you pushed! That's why you're so tired. How did I miss that?"

"Stop. Please, Jess. Just stop."

"I care about you!"

"This is what you wanted. You need to think about that."

Amanda undressed, putting on a pair of shorts and a T-shirt. She climbed into bed and rolled over, giving Jess her back. "Go to sleep," she said softly.

"Just because Finn can't let go doesn't mean you have to hold on, too."

"Go . . . to . . . sleep."

Jess turned off the light and sat in bed, staring across

the room, wondering at the divide that existed there—a space so much bigger than the gap between their beds. For the first time in their life together, something had separated them. That distance felt wider than the Grand Canyon, though to be fair, she'd never seen the Grand Canyon.

Confused and stung by her exclusion, Jess's vision blurred with tears.

"Please?" she whispered.

Amanda didn't speak, just sighed and tugged the sheet higher on her shoulders.

In the dark, her eyes were wide and sad.

"I hate this," Jess said. The words were still swimming around her head when she fell asleep thirty minutes later.

ORLANDO, FLORIDA

22

PHILBY LIKED FINN'S HOUSE. Mrs. Whitman had baked cookies. His own parents could be so annoying, Philby thought, picking a cookie up and taking a giant bite. Not Mrs. Whitman.

They sat in the living room, with its flat-panel TV, comfortable chairs, and view of the street. Finn's sister was doing homework in the kitchen, so they kept their voices down.

"Finn isn't going to tell you this," Philby said to Mrs. Whitman. "Because of your being a rocket scientist and all—"

"I'm retired."

"Mom, I couldn't remember anything after I crossed over." Finn blurted the words out like a confession.

"And that's because?" his mother asked.

Philby cleared his throat, and then ate another cookie, his chewing obscuring his words. "We—that is, the Imagineers . . . Jeez, this is going to sound ridiculous."

"Try me," she said.

"Time travel," Philby spit out. "I know how it sounds! Believe me, I know! But there's evidence, and you being so smart and all, we . . . that is, Finn and me—"

"Finn and I," Mrs. Whitman corrected.

"Mom!" Finn groaned.

"The Imagineers won't tell us what's going on. Not yet, at least. We know they suspect something big. But I think they're so stuck in 'reality' that they can't admit to themselves it might actually be possible to time travel."

"You did make the jump from memory lapse to time travel rather quickly," Mrs. Whitman said, suppressing a smile.

"You don't believe us," Finn said. "I knew this was a stupid idea!" He gave Philby a scornful look. "Figures. I'm still considered a freak by the other Keepers. And they were there. They saw what happened."

"It's on video," Philby said, interrupting Finn's rant. "A seam in the image, like a filmy, oily crack. Then it's gone, and so is Finn." Mrs. Whitman's eyes widened at the mention of her son. "Then, minutes later, it happens again, and Finn reappears." Philby allowed this to sink in. "We're pretty sure it has happened before, but Brad—you know Brad—wouldn't exactly say so. But he didn't deny it, either."

Her eyes darted nervously between the two boys. Then, at last, Mrs. Whitman focused on her son. "This isn't a joke," she said.

Finn shook his head. "Please, Mom. Is it possible?"

"Well, yes. Einstein and others have hypothesized about the exceptional qualities of time, and some of those ideas now appear theoretically accurate. It's been studied and discussed endlessly. Some astronomy supports, even seems to prove, the possibility. But that's all it is. A theory."

"But if it were physically possible," Philby said, "it would involve the speed of light, right?"

"It's theorized in those terms."

"So being a DHI for instance—being pure light—it might be possible."

"Look, boys, there are people who will tell you that fortune tellers and psychics are real, that people can shut their eyes and actually see your future. Others will claim they've been to the future and then traveled back. It's a common delusion among homeless people and the less fortunate. A handful of well-respected scientists believe a small percentage of these transients—'crazies,' you might call them—are not impaired at all, but are simply trying to explain an experience that actually took place." Mrs. Whitman leaned forward in her chair, pressing her palms together and fixed a stare on her son. To Finn, the silence in the room felt absolute. "Kind of like Jess and her dreams."

"No," Finn said. "That is the future. We're talking about the past."

"Okay. So, anyway, you have this group of physicists consistently working to accomplish some of the things Einstein and others theorized," Mrs. Whitman said, "and another group claiming they've experienced these things for real. Then you have the rest of us. Including me. I appreciate the theory, certainly. But do I think my son has gone into the future? No."

"The *past*?" Finn restated. "What about the past?"

Mrs. Whitman smiled patronizingly.

Philby set his third cookie down. "But if we accept that some people may have time traveled, then couldn't we explain them seeming crazy, or even being driven crazy, by the fact that no one believes them?"

"That's what I was just talking about, Dell." Mrs. Whitman didn't sound convinced.

"So what if Wayne figured this out? Let's say he realized that human beings who time travel go nuts. But DHIs, being made of light? Maybe not so much."

"You sure get an A for creativity," Mrs. Whitman said.

"Brad, the Imagineer, couldn't explain what happened to Finn during those missing minutes," Philby said. "Can you?"

She went a shade paler. "Not without seeing the video."

"The Imagineers studied the video. The time

code was uninterrupted, Brad said. There were no edits."

More silence. Above the fireplace, a clock ticked.

"The carousel slowed to a stop once I disappeared. It started up again before I returned," Finn said. "In the video, I just show up back on the horse."

"What carousel?" his mother asked. "What horse?"

"I was on King Arthur Carrousel when I disappeared. Riding the golden horse, like Wayne told me to do in the message we found."

"Oh, for goodness' sake. I'm sorry to say this, Finn, but I'm beginning to side with your father. Enough is enough."

"The carousel started up again just before Finn returned," Philby said.

"Boys! Really!"

"I didn't remember anything!" Finn said again, more desperately this time. "That protects me, Mom. It keeps me from sounding crazy, from going crazy. Wayne protected me."

"You're borderline, believe me." Taking a deep breath, the former rocket scientist addressed Philby, appealing to the computer geek's scientific mind. "It's possible, even probable, that upstream and downstream data are handled differently. Upstream, when Finn crosses over, is less dangerous to a server than is incoming data. So you go out clean; you do whatever you do as DHIs; but then your data are scrubbed for viruses and malware upon your return."

"Affecting memory!" Phiby said.

"Precisely. Corporations take antivirus measures extremely seriously these days. Including Disney. What if data not matching the original outgoing video stream is clipped and deleted from the incoming data stream when Finn returns? That data could represent anything learned, seen, heard, gained."

"I get that, but the thing is, he remembers crossing over, just not the carousel part."

"Could that have been Wayne's intention? It doesn't mean Finn time traveled." Mrs. Whitman threw her hands up in exasperation. "People don't time travel!"

"So Wayne found a way to make him invisible or something like that?" Philby sounded fairly convinced.

"For as smart as you both are, you're missing the point," Finn said.

"Which is?" his mother asked.

"If we accept the idea of antivirus software scrubbing extra data," Finn said to his mother, "or the notion that I went invisible," to Philby, "then what explains this?"

He pulled up his shirt sleeve, displaying the hastily drawn fountain pen on his forearm. The image had faded, but its lines were still visible in the clear daylight. "This was here when the missing minutes were over."

Mrs. Whitman reached out and gently ran her thumb across Finn's skin. It was like she didn't believe the drawing was actually there.

"It's Walt's pen," Finn said. He'd spoken the words so often, but they had never sounded more sincere. His mother knew the history and importance of the pen.

She nodded faintly, suddenly on the verge of tears.

"A message," Finn said.

His mother nodded again, closer than ever to crying. Worried for her son. "I don't know what to believe."

"How can my memories not get through, but a drawing of a pen does? It doesn't make sense, does it, Mom?"

Mrs. Whitman shook her head gently and then looked up at her son, tears welling in her eyes. "Oh, it makes all sorts of sense," she said, "just not the kind you want it to."

Her voice dropped; she spoke so softly that both boys leaned in to hear. "You know what a psychologist would say? She'd say you are so desperate to win back the support of your friends, so eager to prolong a fantasy life that is all but over, that you've convinced yourself you didn't make this up."

Finn sat back, stunned. "What? Mom?"

"You believe us," Philby said, pushing her. "I know you do."

"I know you boys wouldn't lie to me." She looked at her son for a long moment. "Not consciously. But that's not the same thing as believing you."

"Humor me, Mom. Indulge my fantasy and accept that I time traveled. Make it a story in your head—I don't care how. Just explain how this pen ended up drawn onto my arm."

He'd won a faint smile from her. "A story, okay."

"Thank you," Philby said softly.

"Whoever drew that pen wanted to send a message," she said. "He or she knew the pen would mean something to you, that it's significant. That you, Finn, are focused on getting it back onto Walt's desk so that you can find it forty years later and save the day." She shot her son a look. Could he hear how ridiculous this all sounded? Then her voice turned solemn, like a judge commuting a life sentence. "Of course, it's also an invitation. There's an obvious reaction to the pen."

"Which is?" Finn and Philby nearly spoke in unison.

"The next time you cross over," she said to her son, granting him permission to continue the experiment, the tears finally slipping down her cheeks, "you need to carry your own message on the other arm."

23

GIVEN THAT WILLA WAS one half of the "Wilby" pair, she proved susceptible to Philby's pleading for help. He'd asked her to cross over with Finn as far as the King Arthur Carrousel, but no further, to observe in real time what the Imagineers had seen on video. In particular, she was to take a close look at Finn's arms the moment he reappeared on Jingles.

Provided he did reappear.

Finn's recollection of red eyes lurking in shadow, along with the food poisoning incident at their Keepers event, suggested that somehow, impossible though it might seem, the Overtakers had been rejuvenated. Though he felt it was implausible, the potential threat contributed to Philby's decision to carry out their mission during park hours, when an outright attack was less likely.

Because of the phenomenon of the "lint" and "oil" and Finn's disappearance from Jingles, the team decided to cross over in the early evening, after dark, but before park closing. The following day Willa and Finn woke early in order to be tired enough to fall asleep that evening. Once crossed over into Disneyland's Central Plaza, they headed to Walt's apartment. Willa wrote a message in ink on his DHI forearm.

Where am I? What is the date?

Finn wound the music box tight and started the calliope melody. Hurrying to King Arthur Carrousel, he cheated by passing his DHI through the retaining fence, allowing him to cut the twenty-minute line of guests waiting to board the ride. On the carousel, he stood by Jingles, waited for the platform to start moving, and climbed onto the horse. He felt like he was standing at the start line of a huge race, his breath short, his heart in his throat.

From the sidelines, Willa noted the time as eight fifty p.m. She moved as best she could through the crowds, trying to circle the carousel and keep an eye on Finn. But the golden horse outpaced her, and she lost sight of him.

Below the ride's colorful insignia, above the bobbing horses, she saw an anomaly on the far side of the carousel. For a split second, it looked like a cracked mirror, the reflection divided into fragmented pieces. It did, in fact, look like a piece of lint or hair on a movie theater screen.

In the blink of an eye, it was gone, leaving only an oily texture to the air, like heat shimmering off the sidewalk. That, too, melted away, returning clarity of sight.

It all happened so fast that Willa wasn't sure she'd seen anything at all. Not until the carousel came back around and the golden horse stood empty, its rider gone.

A chill struck her, running up her spine. At first, Willa attributed it to Finn's disappearance. But it echoed throughout her body, down her arms, and through her fingers, tickling her toes. She recognized it as the chill of fear. She knew in a sickening instant that someone was watching her.

24

WILLA FELT SICK. It went beyond creepy. It felt dirty and ugly and if it could have smelled, it would have smelled sour and foul.

Finn's disappearance went right out of her head. Taking a deep breath and turning to face Mr. Toad's Wild Ride, she knew the feeling came from there. It was, in fact, one of the darkest of the park's so-called "dark rides," an aimless car trip of destruction that ended in arrest and punishment at the gates of hell. Not exactly kiddie fare.

A flash of red eyes sent more shivers through her. The devil. It had to be! The location, red glowing eyes peering out from shadow—what else?

But she was being ridiculous. The spike of terror triggered both a loss of all clear and a second, somehow more scalding realization: the Overtakers! She and the Keepers had so easily dismissed Finn's suggestions, had chalked them up to the ranting of a grief-stricken boy desperate to cling to the excitement and dangers of the recent past.

It had all been so easy to make fun of. Until now.

If she was right, this was huge. Willa wanted to prove it. She wanted to prevent whatever, whoever this was from hurting Finn when he returned.

She relaxed back to all clear. As a hologram, even a version 1.6, there was little chance of her being harmed if she kept her head.

Charged with determination, she shed her concern, marched over to Mr. Toad's Wild Ride, and entered the empty waiting queue area. ⁂This was a bad idea. A very, very bad idea. She shouldn't have been alone. It was dark. She grimaced with every step.*

Had she been less determined, less singularly focused, she might have noticed the old-fashioned policeman string a rope across the entry behind her, closing the ride.

She reached the boarding area quickly. No Cast Members.

"Hello?"

No answer.

Willa climbed into the waiting car. Though there was no Cast Member at the control stand, the car took off right on schedule. Made no sense. Panic rose in Willa's gut as the safety bar slid into place—but too far, too tight!

---

*Dark_Robinswood

She pushed against it. Trapped! Willa's fear had solidified her hologram; she was pinned to the bench. The car swung through the parting doors ahead, into a dark library where a blue-bearded man threw books at her—actual books. They hit her, and they hurt. That wasn't supposed to happen.

The car jerked quickly to the left. A full suit of armor raised its arm and lowered a battle-ax. Willa, still pinned by the bar, leaned left. The battle-ax cut a slice of the car's plastic siding away. In spite of herself, she screamed.

No! Stop. She reminded herself to push away fear and concern, which were the real enemy of any version 1.6 hologram. But how to do so when she was being jerked and threatened at every turn? The chandelier overhead swayed back and forth, disorienting her.

Suddenly, a bright blue policeman loomed up before her, hand outstretched in warning, and took a swing at her chest. His nightstick smacked her on the arm. Willa cried out. Pinned to the seat. Pitch-black. Another cop leaped forward. He, too, was alive, not the cartoon he should have been. Their faces were terrifying; there was no way for Willa to calm herself. The bar continued to pin her to the seat.

Jerking along the tracks, the car spun into a room of stacked wooden barrels and crates that collapsed forward, falling onto her. The car bumped and jerked and plowed on, but too late: Willa had been hit on the head.

Dazed, hurting, she called out: "Stop! The! Ride!"

The car shot ahead. Horrific colors and explosions erupted around her—*BAM! BOOM!*—reflecting how her head felt. A train locomotive aimed at her car, threatening a head-on collision. Willa closed her eyes and focused until feeling the tingles of being a pure hologram again.

She leaned forward, and moved the restraining bar through her middle.

The train hit her car head-on, smashing it to bits.

The ride's emergency lights switched on. Harsh shadows flickered around her. Willa scrambled and hid just as the set of red eyes reappeared. She cupped her hands over her mouth to keep from screaming. She worked to keep herself pure hologram, hoping her faint blue outline wouldn't give her away.

The eyes blinked.

Deep breath, Willa told herself.

The emergency lights continued flashing on the ceiling. Running footsteps approached. The glowing eyes withdrew.

Willa spotted an exit sign and crawled toward it, not wanting to explain herself or the destruction to the ride.

Overtakers . . .

There was no other explanation.

25

FROM THE MOMENT WILLA emerged from what she'd now be calling Mr. Toad's *Disastrous* Ride, she found herself warmed by the magic of Disneyland. Though she was nowhere near as familiar with this park as she was with Disney World's Magic Kingdom, she found herself reveling in the joy and excitement of the guests. It was the perfect balm after her death-defying ride in Mr. Toad's car—and a huge relief from the renewed terror of the Overtakers.

She carefully watched the carousel for any sign of Finn. Jingles was occupied on every new run. Keeping her hologram back to the wall directly beneath where she believed the security camera was located, Willa poked at the bruises on her arms, worried they would carry over when she returned. She was going to look a mess.

Still, she was buoyed by a sense of accomplishment at having defied Mr. Toad's devilish intentions—and determined to remain on high alert for other attacks. Finn's report of the red eyes watching him took on new meaning. What if a character from Mr. Toad's was an Overtaker keeping watch on the carousel?

But for what? For whom? And most importantly: *why?*

Casting her eyes about the crowd, Willa caught a glimpse of a stranger's wristwatch. Twenty minutes had passed since Finn's disappearance. She surveyed the area again, spotting a pair of men she knew to be Cryptologists, members of a secretive Imagineering group. Responsible for monitoring the Overtakers, their presence at the carousel could not be considered coincidence. Neither could their staring at her.

They, too, were awaiting Finn's return.

This made things more complicated. First, the appearance of an Overtaker threat in Mr. Toad's. Now, Finn's allies wanting a piece of him. It all seemed to support Finn's claims, claims that she and the other Keepers had been mocking for weeks. Months!

Riven by guilt, feeling like the worst of all possible friends, Willa schemed out what to do next. As much as she and the Keepers valued the Cryptos, she wanted to protect Finn from them. *Hurry up!* she urged silently, shouting the words in her mind, sensing time was working against them. She'd left Mr. Toad's devil none too happy. If he were keeper of the carousel, he might have plans of his own for Finn.

When one of the Cryptos started toward her, Willa moved away. The Keepers weren't allowed to use DHI technology without the Imagineers' permission. Philby had been crossing them over for years illegally. He'd even built them their own Return for these manual crossings. At a distance, the Crypto wouldn't be able to ascertain Willa's current state, but if he got close enough, the faint blue 1.6 outline would give her away. Everyone would be in trouble.

Waiting parents and families formed a human apron around King Arthur Carrousel, providing Willa with good cover. She moved between people, using them like tree trunks in the forest, keeping screens between herself and the Crypto coming after her. All this while still rising frequently to her tiptoes to keep an eye on Jingles.

A flash of movement—as if there weren't enough on her plate. Pain and Panic were visible in the near distance, also circling in toward her. Minions of Hades—a.k.a., the Devil—she couldn't recall ever having seen them as characters in the parks. *So why now?* Willa was fairly certain she knew the answer, but it wasn't an answer she wanted. If her DHI could be made to panic, she would be vulnerable.

Willa dealt with these many variables as a juggler would—she kept her eye on one thing, allowing practice to take care of the rest. She kept her attention on Jingles, and her optimistic expectation that Finn would soon return.

26

Unseen by Willa, behind her the Crypto gestured broadly to his partner, indicating Pain and Panic. The presence of the two characters in the park raised the alarm. Any unusual sighting held significance. Having nearly reached Willa, the Crypto changed course to intercept Pain and Panic. His co-worker did the same.

"Can I help you?" the Crypto called out.

Pain and Panic turned.

"Help?" Pain asked. "We are the ones who give the help! Never the other way around!"

Panic nodded cartoonishly. "Yup. Yup."

Pain engaged his counterpart. "Has anyone ever offered to help us? And by 'ever,' I mean 'on any occasion, under any circumstances, on any account?'"

"Nope. Nope."

"Then don't you think we ought to thank the man?"

"I think we ought to thank the man."

Before the Imagineer could step back, the two minions grabbed him at the same time. His eyes went wide with fright, shockingly large in his instantly bloodless face, and he shivered under a rush of pain so intense his vocal cords locked and his lungs froze. Silently, he dropped to his knees, Pain still grasping him by the arm. As the character released him, he keeled over.

When Panic reached down and patted his cheek like a caring mother, the Crypto shook head to toe. Quickening their pace, the two characters closed the distance with Willa. Their smiles were nothing short of pure evil.

27

THE AIR SHIMMERED LIKE OIL above the carousel horse. A crack tore open the air like a black scar. Finn appeared, straddling the rump of Jingles. He rode just behind a young pigtailed princess.

To Willa, Finn looked like a person awakened too quickly from a deep sleep. Disoriented. Dislodged. She could see him try to collect his bearings, to make sense of it all.

A woman—most likely the princess's mother—cried out, and tried to pull Finn off Jingles. Her hand moved right through the young man. She froze in disbelief. Her second try caught a compromised DHI. Made mortal and material by confusion, Finn was knocked off the horse. The woman snatched her child in her arms, and ran.

A Crypto headed in Willa's direction. She couldn't locate the man's partner. Worried he was about to blindside her, she took the offensive.

"Look!" she called out loudly. "An Imagineer!" She pointed at the Crypto. The crowd responded, enthusiastically. It surrounded her pursuer, slowing him. Willa took a calming breath and pushed her DHI *through* every obstacle in her way, starting with the people, and then a planter and finally a railing. She timed it well, pulling a woozy Finn up off the floor of the slowing carousel. She hauled him off, and into the crowd.

There were whispers of "Kingdom Keeper," her name and Finn's. Faint applause. The Imagineer called for her to stop.

"You good?"

Finn nodded, still dazed.

"Faster!" she urged.

Finn got his feet under him and began running on his own.

Willa caught a glimpse of Finn's left forearm, pumping furiously as he ran. If they weren't being chased by an Imagineer (she was), and he wasn't being pursued in turn by a pair of evil cartoon characters (he was), she might have stopped Finn to study the additional writing on Finn's arm.

She managed to pick out numbers—*1313* and *471*.

But that was all. The rest would have to wait.

As she and Finn reached Disneyland's Central Plaza, their pursuers nearly upon them, Finn looked at her, puzzlement still muddying his eyes.

"I remember stuff!" he said.

She stopped him at the base of the Partners statue.

𐌻𐌺Fingerprints of an artist's touch encompassed every surface of the statue, the castle looming behind.* Wrapping one arm around him, she did something that—amazingly!—she'd never done before.

She pushed the button.

---

*Stonecutter_Cannon

28

THE KEEPERS MET in the local skateboard park Finn had frequented as a middle schooler. Finn hadn't told his mother he was leaving the house, but it was before his curfew of eleven p.m., so technically he didn't feel he had to.

Like Finn, Willa was still in the clothes she'd been wearing when they'd crossed over. Philby's loose-fitting gray T-shirt, shorts, and sandals made him look like a surfer dude. His red hair was tousled, his smile a little forced. They stood under one of the bright lights that lit the park in silver cones. Mist hung in the cool evening air.

"Can I see it?" Philby asked, taking Finn's left arm before his friend could grant him permission. "Bizarre," he said softly, tracing his fingers across the words written there.

set to 13/3
bring file IAV-471

"Weird, right?" Finn said. "And I know what you're

going to say, but I'm telling you: that's not my hand-writing."

"It was there on his arm when I pulled him off Jingles," Willa confirmed. "Wherever he was, whatever happened to him, he came back with that message."

"Which means we owe you an apology." Maybeck stepped from the shadows and joined them under the light. He and Finn exchanged fist bumps, but the famil-iar ritual was more solemn, somehow. "I thought you'd gone mental, man. Seriously."

"How did you—?"

"I called him," Willa said. "I told him about Mr. Toad's *Nearly Fatal* Ride, the Cryptos. Pain and Panic."

"We . . . I . . . the thing is . . ." Maybeck stuttered, seeming to not know what to say.

"No problem." Finn took mercy on him. "This may sound strange, but I didn't want to believe it, either. Not really. To go through everything we went through, to lose Dillard and Wayne, and then to have it all start again? All I wanted . . . but forget it; we're past that."

"We were jerks. We *are* jerks," Maybeck said. "So much for one-for-all-and-all-for-one. We left you hanging."

Philby still held Finn's left arm. Again and again, he traced the blurry letters, his eyes distant. "IAV. I know that tag. 'Imagineers Audio Visual.' It goes way back. Hasn't been used since the nineteen sixties."

"So what's in file four-seven-one?" Willa asked.

"No idea. But someone needs that file." Philby sounded concerned.

"What's with 'bring'?" Finn chimed in.

"You're the only one who can answer that. What happened to you after you got onto Jingles?"

"I actually do remember some stuff," Finn said. "A stage. Lights. Audio-Animatronics. A guy older than us but too young to be anybody important. I think maybe the guy wrote it on my arm. I'm not sure." He checked with Philby. "This is where you're supposed to think I'm crazy."

"Your mother made sure that wouldn't happen," Philby said. "Now, I don't know what to think."

"I remember being rescued by Willa. Thank you for that, by the way."

Willa shook her head. "You were gone for more than twenty minutes."

"Seriously? No real memory of that."

"The lint?" Philby asked Willa.

She nodded. "Yup. Both times, leaving and returning. It's much more vivid in person."

"Oh, man. Are we talking time travel again?" Maybeck asked. He was with them, but only so far. "It's gotta be an illusion. Right? A magic trick! Think about magicians. They can make elephants disappear. Finn would be a piece of cake."

"And the loss of memory could be the result of hypnotism." Willa sounded relieved, excited.

"It is a much more reasonable explanation," Philby said.

"So, you're saying Wayne did all this so I could be hypnotized," Finn said, raising an eyebrow. "The hypnotist, this magician guy, wrote something on my arm, and meanwhile the Overtakers put on a little show just so Willa wouldn't be bored?"

"Well, if you put it like that," Philby said, "it sounds plain stupid."

"I'm doing it again, huh?" Maybeck said. "Not believing you."

"I did not write this message," Finn said, meeting their eyes one by one. His look was calm, steady. "I don't even know what it means. And I don't think my vanishing off that horse was an illusion. Yes, hypnotism could erase my memory—but dang, you guys, aren't we past that?"

"We need to find this file," Philby said, finally releasing Finn's arm.

"Thirteen thirteen is the street address of Disneyland." Willa paused, then added, "I'm just saying."

A prolonged silence spread through the four friends.

"It's Wayne," Finn said. "Don't ask me how, but it's definitely Wayne."

"We need to find the file." Philby's firm tone left no room for argument.

"I'll bet Amanda and Jess would help," Finn said. "Especially if you asked, Philby. They're out there. They're part of the company now. They find it, I deliver it."

There had been a time when Finn might have struggled with confronting Philby, might have worried it would start a turf war between the two. Not any longer. Since the epic battle in Disneyland, the Keepers had forged what had felt like an inseparable team. The rest of them bailing on Finn had scarred his heart, but his faith in the team as a whole had not waivered.

"I'll contact Amanda again," Philby said. "I agree. That keeps it a business relationship." He directed this at Finn. "You sure that's okay?"

Finn winced a smile. "I'm not sure of anything."

ANAHEIM, CALIFORNIA

The Tower Dorm

29

TIM SOUNDED LIKE a game show host. "Amanda, I'd like you to meet—"

"Emily," Amanda said, interrupting Tim. "We met earlier, you idiot! In the library."

Tim rolled his eyes at her name-calling. Ignoring him, Amanda spun around in the center of Emily's bedroom, taking in the fantastic space. "It's so pretty!" she cried.

"Thanks."

Decorated in colorful fabrics, Emily's dorm room created the effect of being inside a sultan's tent. Parachute silk draped a dome light. Scarves and pieces of clothing were hung as art on the parachute walls. The only paper art was a *Catching Fire* poster on the wall beside Emily's roommate's bed.

"It's called wearable art. And that's my deal," Emily said.

"Including new fabric technologies," Tim said, nudging her.

"For Tim," Emily said, rolling her eyes, "everything's technology."

"Let's say," Tim eased the door shut and spoke cautiously, "that a person or persons had good reason to want to get past some video cams. Could a certain other person, who just happened to have chosen enrollment in DSI over a Defense Department job, be able to help?"

Emily looked suddenly serious. "I think the certain other person would want to know what the person or persons had in mind. For instance, what kind of trouble would she be in if they get caught? Robbing a bank for instance, is just plain wrong."

"No banks," Tim said.

"It's a file, a very important file, that a friend of mine, a good friend, was told is in the school archives," Amanda explained. "His name is Dell Philby. He's one of the Kingdom—"

"Keepers? No way! You know those guys?"

"I do. Which is why it's super important."

Tim stayed silent, but he looked impressed as well. In spite of herself, Amanda felt pride tickling the base of her spine, pushing her to smile. At the DSI, no heroes were more lauded and admired than the Kingdom Keepers.

Fighting back a smile, Amanda explained. "Jess and I have met them a couple times." She downplayed the depth of their relationships for now. "Philby knows I'm here at DSI. He spoke with Becky—"

"Cline. Studio Archives. Are you some kind of VIP or something?" Emily sounded overly impressed. This was what Jess had wanted to avoid—the star treatment phenomenon.

"Not me. Them. The Keepers. Becky told Philby the information we need is almost certainly stored here in the dorm basement, but that it's part of a classified file she can't get."

"So we're going to steal classified files?" Emily asked.

"I like that 'we' part!" Tim said.

"I'm going to *borrow* them," Amanda said. "I'll either take photos or copy them, and then put them right back."

"And you're going to take this risk because . . . ?"

"What are friends for?" Amanda forced a smile. "Actually, the Keepers pretty much saved the life of a friend of mine. I kind of owe them big time."

"Jess," Tim stated, though in a private, caring way.

Amanda didn't answer.

Emily didn't look convinced. Crossing her arms across her chest, her face shadowed by pink light shining through the fabric dome, she addressed Tim. "Why me?"

"The Chameleon project."

"No way."

"Em, we have to. Have you ever heard of a three-ninety?"

"The robots?" Emily asked. "Of course. We studied those. They were decommissioned."

"Yeah, well, apparently, not all of them. Amanda and I met a few earlier. Highly modified." Tim showed her the red mark on his arm where he'd been shocked. "Highly *dangerous*."

"You've been down there?" Emily stiffened, suddenly seeming more interested. "The three-nineties have video, right?"

"Yeah, but lo-res. They do have lateral servos but they can't see much below two feet off the floor."

Keenly interested in the information Tim was supplying, Emily moved to her desk and started punching keys on her open laptop. "Okay. The lighting down there?"

Tim said, "Fluorescent and compact fluorescent."

Emily typed. "No LED or incandescent?"

"Nope."

Emily clicked through several links. "The specs conform."

"What's going on?" Amanda asked.

"A little something Em calls 'Chameleon.'" Tim looked impossibly self-satisfied.

"I could explain it," Emily said, "if you'd completed

the Applied Physics and Electrical Dynamics course."

"Last semester, first year," Tim explained, and then added mock condescendingly, "You'll get there."

"Chameleon," Amanda repeated.

Emily pursed her lips. "The current rage is smart textiles: weaving electronic and optic fibers into wearables."

"Em's specialty," Tim said. "Her term paper was *Weaving the Past Into the Future*."

"I didn't know you'd read my paper."

"It was used for our final exam in Expressions of Light. Robertson called it 'brilliant.'" Tim smiled, showing his teeth. "But don't let it go to your head."

"I'm still not getting it," Amanda said.

"The concept's easy." Emily spun her laptop so Amanda could see the screen and computer art of a full bodysuit made of hundreds of small gray disks. It looked like something a scuba diver would wear. "Cameras, good cameras, have shrunk to the size of pinheads. Think about the backup cameras on your parents' car."

"I don't have parents." Amanda blurted it out. It had become habit, though she immediately regretted it as it sounded like she was playing the pity card.

Emily looked as if she might say something in response, then returned her attention to her laptop. Amanda appreciated that. "The going theory is, you integrate a few cameras with imaging technology. Thanks to fiber optics, it all happens at close to the speed of light. What a camera sees on one side of the suit"—she tapped the trackpad, setting the animation in motion—"is instantly projected to the other." With a click of the mouse, the suit all but disappeared, taking on the pattern of the wallpaper behind it. A gray smudge remained on the side, from the armpit to below the hips. "Now, it would be pretty simple technology if human beings were two dimensional, but seeing as we're not, it takes pretty sophisticated algorithms to ensure that whichever side the object is seen from"—the suit rotated to a side view and the gray smudge became more solid, like a gray line drawn down the wallpaper pattern—"the background is projected correctly. It is less than perfect at the moment."

"But operational," Tim added.

"Like Harry Potter's cloak," Amanda said.

"But for real," added Tim.

"Invisibility?" Amanda gasped, bringing her hand to her mouth. She could move objects with her mind, but this seemed beyond even her admittedly big suspension of disbelief. "Too cool."

"I have a sample," Emily said. She dug around in her closet and retrieved a gray piece of fabric the size of a dinner napkin. A pair of extremely thin wires ran from the fabric to a black box the size of a deck of cards. Emily plugged in the box and said, "Tim? Hold it, please?"

Tim took the sample, holding it parallel to Emily's bed and the fabric art behind it—a sunset made completely of colored pieces of cloth. The napkin blocked Amanda's view of the wall. Emily threw a switch on the box, and . . .

The wall art reappeared. Only when Tim pinched the napkin did any clue to the invisibility fabric's existence show.

"That's crazy!" Amanda breathed.

"Em's been working on wearable prototypes for Chameleon, haven't you, Em?"

"I have two finished. Both women's, both my size. *Our* size," she said, looking carefully at Amanda. They were roughly the same height, with similar builds. "We girls have to reduce our curves as much as possible. So I've built Spanx into the bottoms, and we can wrap our tops tight. Curves make things extremely complex. Because of that, in a must-not-be-seen situation, it's better to face the person or animal viewing you, front or back, not to the side."

"Person, animal . . . or video camera," Tim added. Emily smiled at him, taking the napkin back and turning off the battery pack.

"But how do you power it?" Amanda said.

"You wear two packs, here." Emily indicated a point high up the inside of her thighs. "One is power, the other's circuitry. Battery's good for just over ten minutes right now. No longer than twelve. That's one of the big limitations."

Amanda considered what she was hearing. They couldn't know that she'd seen so many impossible things happen that this actually made sense. She wondered why Tim was so willing to help her. She didn't like the idea of being in debt to anyone.

"You want me to wear this thing to avoid the three-nineties?" Amanda asked. "What's in it for you?"

"I'm just such a nice guy."

"You want me to get something for you while I'm there."

"Of course! If possible. I realize it's dangerous. I'm not expecting miracles."

"It is dangerous," Amanda said, shifting her eyes pointedly to Emily. "Tell her."

Tim recounted their earlier exploits, holding back nothing, including Dirk's final malevolent pursuit and their near escape in the dumbwaiter.

"If you're caught," Tim told Emily, "you'll both be suspended or expelled."

"Yeah," Emily said, enthusiasm evident on her face,

"but if we're *not* caught, then my prototypes will have passed a legit field test, and I move to the top of my class."

"You don't want to do this," Amanda said softly. She had a feeling it would be impossible to convince Emily, but she wanted to try. "You can coach me and I can do this by myself."

"Of course you can." Emily's voice oozed sarcasm. "But there's no way that's going to happen. Now, let's get you fitted."

30

"HOW DOES IT FEEL?" Emily asked Amanda.

"You're littler than I am, but if I don't breathe, I'm okay," Amanda said. She and Emily laughed.

"You both look like Spider-Man," Tim said. "Only you're girls and your costumes are, like, scales. Or tiny gray sequins. So maybe not so much."

"Miniature LEDs," Emily said, correcting him. "Like the world globe in Epcot's Reflections of Earth."

The three were crammed into the small third floor maintenance room that housed the pair of dumbwaiters.

"It may be lunchtime up here, but it'll feel like midnight down there," Tim said. "You need to be back on the afternoon shuttle for classes at DSI. That gives you less than an hour."

"Tim, what makes you think the dumbwaiters will work? I'm ninety-nine-percent sure Dirk knows we used them."

"As far as he knows, he disabled them," Tim said, a little too proudly, "which is completely excellent for us, since in all my brilliance, I overrode his effort. In his mind, there's no way these can operate, which means you should be safe upon landing, as well as for takeoff."

Emily emitted a soft laugh. "They do not make a hat big enough for your head." Turning awkwardly in the cramped space, she addressed Amanda, their faces very close together. "Remember, the Chameleons have a two-foot minimum focal range, so try to keep everything more than an arm's distance away from you. Oh, and my suit has a few extra effects. Don't be startled if I use them."

"Okay," Amanda said, feeling a new burst of nerves creep through her.

"Obviously we'll only use the suits when needed," Emily cautioned. "Ten minutes goes by incredibly fast. Don't throw the switch unless you have to. Even turned off, the suits are hard to see in low light."

"Got it."

"Ready?"

"Ready."

They climbed together into one dumbwaiter, packing in as tightly as they could. Tim pulled down the grate, threw them a mini-salute, and wished them good luck.

* * *

Minutes later, the two girls crossed the laundry room. Amanda pointed out the short-circuited 390 lying in the doorway. But the other doorway stood empty.

Emily kept her voice down. "Seeing the mess down here, I guess I should mention something else. The suits have to stay clean. Dirt or mud on the diodes shows up as a black spot or lines. I call them dead spots. Not good."

Shuddering at the thought, Amanda gave a thumbs-up. She carefully cleared a path through the mess of spilled detergent with a rag. The girls stepped over the 390 and out of the laundry room.

Amanda led the way down the aisle. Things went well until a rat crossed their path and Emily screamed. Both girls froze. Amanda hand signaled, steering them to the left on tiptoes.

A few more minutes passed before a turn left them facing a wall of chain link fence, like a tennis court. The storage area? Amanda wondered. As the girls moved closer, Amanda identified the sound of a 390. She signaled Emily by marching in place mechanically.

Emily nodded and tried the doorknob. Locked. "We're going to stand out of the way. Remember," she whispered, "face it head on. Don't turn to the side."

Amanda nodded.

"Okay. Throw the switch."

The two girls reached down.

They disappeared.

An old man—Dirk—appeared first. He swung a flashlight in front of his path. He was followed by a slower moving 390. As the pair drew nearer, Amanda felt sweat running down her ribs. She hoped she wouldn't short-circuit the suit.

The man's wrinkled leathery eyes squinted. Reaching the door, Dirk stopped and tested it, finding it locked. He turned his back on the chain link and took several steps as if leaving. Then, reconsidering, he withdrew a cluttered key chain, and unlocked the door. The hinges shrieked like wounded birds. In a creaky voice, Dirk called out a command to the waiting robot. "Guard."

The robot issued a series of cheeps.

Dirk entered the room and threw the light switch. Though it was tempting, Amanda did not turn her head to see what he did next. All she could make out was Dirk's shadow, stretching thinly toward the 390.

The invisible Emily took Amanda by the hand and tugged.

The girls slipped in behind Dirk and stopped to face him as he pivoted. He looked directly at them. *Through* them.

He turned down a narrow aisle between tall shelves neatly ordered with hundreds of cardboard file boxes.

Emily pulled Amanda away and down a different aisle. She switched off her suit to conserve the battery. Amanda did the same.

The girls were visible.

31

GAPS BETWEEN THE BOXES afforded Amanda a glimpse of Dirk as he moved slowly down a far aisle. He moved cautiously.

"Who's there?" croaked the old man dryly, almost as if he'd felt her staring. He moved toward them.

Amanda flipped on her suit's invisibility feature. She looked toward Emily. Gone.

Dirk stood at the end of Amanda's aisle. Keeping her shoulders square, she backed up. At the other end, she side-stepped out of sight. She was about to make herself visible again when Dirk called out, "I know you're in here! I will catch you and you will be expelled. These records are off limits!"

Battery or not, she couldn't bring herself to risk being seen.

Dirk crossed into the next aisle over, moving slowly and quietly. Amanda reached for one of the boxes, prepared to give him a start. Dirk, one aisle over, drew closer.

A thought occurred to her. She felt a little devilish as she raised her hands, palms out, and *pushed*.

A dozen boxes, full of binders and papers, went flying into the next aisle.

Dirk pedaled backward and fell over. Gulping and gasping for air, he crawled on hands and knees toward the door.

"Away with you!" he shouted.

Though part of Amanda felt bad about terrifying an old man, she nearly laughed as Emily threw more paperwork into the air. Needing no further incentive, Dirk fled the archive. The hinges cried out as the door banged shut. Amid his scrambling flight, Dirk shouted to the 390, "Stand down! Follow!" and the robot obediently ground its way after him, vacating the room.

A grinning Emily reappeared from invisibility. Amanda switched off her suit.

"That was genius!" Emily said, her eyes aglow. "The entire aisle at once? Using telekinesis? Tina was right?"

"Did you see him run?" Amanda said, avoiding a direct answer.

At her evasion, Emily looked crestfallen. "Oh, I see."

"It's a mess!" Amanda looked around, suddenly sensing the consequences of what she'd done. "How will we find anything now? And keep from getting caught?"

"Don't freak. Here's the trick: if we pick up *all this mess* and put it back, he won't believe it ever happened."

"That's just cruel."

"No, it's important. He'll report this, Amanda. But if we make him look nuts, then this place doesn't get locked up like a prison."

"That doesn't seem fair."

"You can't always play fair. Didn't you learn that from your Keeper friends? Look, he took off scared. People who are scared take a few minutes to get it together. I'll pick up the spilled stuff. You find the files—the ones you want and what Tim's after. But we've got to hurry! At some point he's going to convince himself he shouldn't be so freaked out, and that means he'll come back."

"You sure?"

"Go!"

Amanda sorted out the filing system with relative ease. After that, it was a matter of moving row to row in search of the IAV file Philby wanted. She actually found what Tim was looking for first. With those files in hand, she moved two rows over and located a box on the bottom shelf. Inside, she identified not one, but two 471 files: a and b. She hurried to Emily with the various folders in hand.

"What do I do with these?" she asked.

"Turn around, I'll unzip you."

A moment later, the files shoved against her skin, Amanda felt all the more squished by the suit. It wouldn't zip all the way, but Emily arranged Amanda's hood to cover the gap.

In a stroke of luck, the doorknob to the archives room could be unlocked from the inside. The two girls relocked it upon leaving. With the noise of the hinges now behind them, they reached the basement's main aisle just as Dirk appeared.

At his side was a dark-suited businessman.

The girls switched on their suits. Amanda felt Emily's warm hand on the back of her arm, guiding her forward, keeping her shoulders square. Amanda, uncomfortable with the concept of her own invisibility, nearly screamed as she recognized the businessman.

Tobias Langford.

Emily turned Amanda at the last moment. The girls pivoted like a gate opening. The men passed through seamlessly.

But then Amanda sneezed without warning.

Both men spun around.

"You see? I told you!" Dirk said. "Ghosts!"

"Not possible!" said Langford.

"I'm telling you . . . it's the Hunchback. Like last time!" Dirk sounded ready to cry. He pulled at his hair, twisting the wiry white strands every which way.

"Impossible." Langford shook his head sharply. "We took care of him."

"One of the resident ghosts, then."

"Do you know how much money we paid Lockwood and Company to get rid of those things? The ghosts are gone, Dirk. They're nothing but a story now. An old story no one believes."

"I've been telling you all for years that they're still down here."

Amanda felt Emily's hand tighten convulsively on her arm. She looked down—and choked back a gasp. Large spots on her suit, spots the size of buttons, were flashing gray. Her battery was failing. The sputtering LEDs formed ripples across her suit, a movement like water.

"You see that?" Dirk spit out. "What is that?"

He edged closer, reluctantly. Transfixed by her failing suit, Amanda failed to step back.

Dirk bumped into her hip.

But then Amanda felt herself pulled—Emily!—and a pair of arms wrapped around her. Resolutely, Emily marched Amanda ahead, her toes nudging Amanda's heels forward. It was a good but flawed attempt. Langford and Dirk saw floating blobs of gray moving away from them, hovering weirdly in the dim air of the basement.

"What—what *is* that?" Langford breathed.

"What did I tell you?" said Dirk. "Ghosts!"

189

Emily hurried Amanda down an aisle, released her, and then they ran. Hard. At the end of the aisle, they turned left, then right; hurled themselves through the laundry room door and jumped over the fallen 390. Breathing hard, they ran for the dumbwaiters—and stopped, frozen in their tracks.

"If we use the dumbwaiter, they'll absolutely know we're real!" Amanda whispered. "You made Chameleon for class, Emily! Langford will figure out it was you."

Cursing under her breath—just like Tim, Amanda thought wryly—Emily pulled Amanda toward a line of cabinets across the room. Both girls crawled inside, pulled the cabinet doors shut, and switched off their suits, conserving what little battery power remained.

The louvered cabinet doors made it possible to see out. The door creaked and Langford stepped into the dark laundry room, his phone extended, casting out light before it as a flashlight.

"What is this place?" Langford said, his voice echoing eerily.

"The old laundry."

"My God, talk about spooky."

"The three-nineties followed whoever was down here into this room. Earlier, I'm talking about. Blue sneakers."

"What's that?"

"I saw a pair of sneakers on the dumbwaiter. Blue sneakers. Big ones. You put your DSI kids in front of me, I can pick 'em out."

"Spend some time upstairs tomorrow. Keep your eyes open." Langford sounded bored and dismissive, but Amanda couldn't tell if he was faking it.

"But what about the ghosts? I'm telling you, Mr. L., you've got to see the records room. Let me show you the mess they made in the records room."

"Yeah. Okay." Langford glanced around the laundry once more. Amanda saw him look directly at the cabinet, at her. She held her gloved hand across her mouth to keep from giving herself away. "I'm telling you, Dirk, what we saw back there was weird. Those shadows, like something melting. Hard to explain."

"Ghosts *are* hard to explain."

"Don't start, Dirk."

"You know as well as I do that strange things have been happening down here for years. Ever since the fire."

"We took care of all that a long time ago. The voices. The crying."

"We ain't seen nothing like this."

"No, Dirk," said Langford, still eyeing the cabinet door. "Nothing like this."

32

"So?" BURIED JUST BELOW Tim's eagerness to hear their report was envy over the girls' accomplishments.

Emily and Amanda sat on a pair of beanbags in the dorm's third-floor game room. The scuffs and thumps of Ping-Pong and foosball competed with the Disney movie sound tracks blasting from the karaoke machine. The acoustic tile ceiling had pencils stuck into it like stalactites, evidencing years of DSI occupancy. The rest of the dorms could seem formal, but this was a relaxed, easy space.

"We got the files," Amanda said.

"Can I see them?" Tim dragged a leaking beanbag over to join them. His long, lanky frame looked awkward stretched out like that. As he wiggled to get comfortable, small plastic balls belched from a tear and bounced away across the floor.

"We weren't able to get yours."

"Please?" he said nicely, his hand outstretched.

Amanda held the files close to her heart, just out of his reach. "Only if you share everything. No more holding back."

"Agreed."

"The shuttle leaves in ten minutes," Emily reminded them.

Tim snatched the files and began reading, turning pages quickly, his perusal punctuated by furtive glances at the two girls. He read faster and faster. His pace frantic, in a race against the clock.

Then his eyes widened. He grinned.

"What?" Amanda asked.

"Why does your friend Philby want this?"

"He didn't say. Only that Finn . . . that the Keepers needed them. Why, *what* are they? What's in there?"

"Detailed specifications of color television transmission."

"Meaning?"

"It's a paint-by-numbers plan for setting up radio towers and broadcasting tri-band color signals. I'll have to check the dates, but by the look of it, it's way ahead of its time. That means the rumors are true!" Tim's eyes glowed triumphantly. "The Imagineers were onto this stuff way ahead of anyone else."

"Jess!" Amanda called out, seeing her for the first time. Across the room, her fellow Fairlie gave an awkward wave, tossed back her pale hair.

Behind Jess, Langford and Dirk were approaching. Amanda struggled out of the beanbag.

Jess reached Tim, bent as if to kiss him on the cheek, stunning Amanda—*totally unlike her!*—and, clearly, Tim. Jess moved past Tim to be a spectator of the foosball match.

Amanda had never seen Jess kiss anyone, never mind a virtual stranger, never mind as theatrically as she just had. It had been a performance. *Why?*

Casting her eyes down, she saw that Tim no longer held the two folders. What had he—

"Mr. Walters! A moment?" Langford's authoritative voice stopped both the Ping-Pong and foosball games. Everyone in the room froze, looking at Tim.

Jess had used the fake kiss to get close enough to Tim in order to snatch the folders away from him. She'd done so just moments ahead of Langford's unannounced arrival. Jess kept the files hidden, her back to the two men.

"Yes, sir?" Tim pulled himself up. He stood a full three inches taller than Langford.

"We'd like to take a look at your closet prior to your boarding the shuttle."

"My closet?"

"Do we have a hearing problem, Mr. Walters?" Langford said distastefully.

"Them blue shoes," said Dirk, and won a belittling look from Langford.

"No problem," Tim said. He glanced at Emily, then Amanda. Panic.

Forcing a smile, Tim joined the two men.

Clearly distressed, Langford next addressed Emily. "Miss Fredrikson? How's that cloaking project of yours coming along? Extra credit, wasn't it?"

"It was—is—yes, extra credit," Emily croaked out, adding awkwardly, "Bernie's my adviser."

"Yes. I hear it's coming along nicely. *Very* nicely."

Recovering herself, Emily said, "I guess. It isn't fully operational yet."

"Oh, really? I've heard differently." Langford smiled tightly, his lips pressed together in a thin line. "Bernie is quite impressed. I think I'd appreciate a demonstration. This evening, perhaps, after classes. Before dinner?"

Dirk's intense stare had not yet left Emily. Amanda shuddered; it was so disturbing.

And Langford's scrutiny swung finally to her.

"You, young lady, are aware that certain areas of the hotel, the dorm, are out of bounds without passes, yes? That venturing into these areas without permission can, *and will*, result in immediate expulsion."

"Yes, sir," Amanda said. "We were told the rules during orientation."

"Being told is one thing. Hearing quite another. I suggest you learn to *listen*, Miss Lockhart."

Amanda nodded again. "Yes, sir."

"I needn't remind you that there's a long line of well-qualified applicants on our waiting list." His gaze swung back to Emily. "That goes for you, too. Seniority in the program will not protect you."

"No, sir," Amanda and Emily said, speaking almost in unison.

"Enough. 'Toby' will do. Remember, Amanda, we're all colleagues here at DSI."

In stark contrast to Langford's words, Tim walked off with the two men like an inmate being escorted down Death Row.

33

LATER, AS THEY WALKED TOGETHER down the central hallway of DSI's Technical Resources and Applications department, Amanda pulled Jess aside and into an empty classroom. Jess untucked her shirt and handed Amanda the two folders.

"I had no idea *what* you were doing."

"It was an air kiss, nothing more, I *promise* you."

"It was brilliant!"

It was the first chance they'd had to talk since arriving at the school building; Jess had jumped onto the dorm shuttle van seconds before its door had closed. She'd ridden in the front with girls Amanda didn't know.

"Why did you disappear like that?" Amanda inquired.

"To get rid of his blue Converse," Jess said, as if it were obvious. "I found Tim's sneakers and disposed of them. Threw them out the window. I ended up out there, too, on the fire escape, but I got rescued by Miles. Do you know him? Tallish, red-brown hair, cute? He let me use his room to make my exit."

"You saved Tim, Jess! I had no idea."

"That's a bit overly dramatic."

"I thought you weren't going to get involved?"

"I thought you and Finn were a thing." Jess narrowed her eyes—and then abruptly looked away, her lips twisted bitterly. Amanda blinked, confused.

"What's that supposed to mean?"

Jess stared fixedly at the wall clock. "Whatever. Look, I don't want to be late for class."

"Jess! What is that supposed to mean?"

^{ᴊᴋ}Jess had tried to dismiss it, telling herself that Amanda and Tim were just new, instant friends. But that had all changed when they'd returned from the basement. Amanda was all best buds, all flirty with Tim, keeping Jess out of it because she'd refused to play along.

For the first time in their shared lives Jess had seen Amanda as competition, and it felt awful. She knew what Amanda was trying to do: punish her for not agreeing to break the rules.

Emotions flooded her. Hate and love. Clarity and confusion. And anger, strongest of all. It bubbled up inside of Jess until she was ready to explode. The only way her body had found to express the pent-up bitterness and resentment was through a single tear that traced its way down her cheek unexpectedly. She felt humiliated for letting that happen.*

---

*Ladder_Finn

"Jessie?" Amanda said, seeing her crying.

"Don't."

"What did I do?"

"Really?"

"Really!"

"It's not the first time, you know. It's just the first time it mattered."

"The first time?" Amanda blinked once, then again, finally getting it. "Tim? Oh, come on, Jess! Seriously? Me and Tim? No, no, no! You made a point of not going with us! And you were the one who saved him by tossing the sneakers. I can't compete with that!" She blinked again, almost laughing from her sheer bafflement. "I *don't want to compete* with that."

"Have you happened to see the way he looks at you?"

"Gimme a break. I could say the same thing."

"You get all the breaks, Amanda. Believe me! *All.*"

"You are totally wrong about this, Jessie."

"Do not call me that! I'm not taking anything any way. Stuff like this, it can't be undone, you know? You can't *push* it back into place." Jess stole another look at the clock. "Whatever. Look, we're going to be late for class."

"Jess! Please!"

Jess left the room, simmering with rage. Amanda repeatedly called out her name through a tight throat, but the door eased shut on its automatic hinge.

Leaving her alone.

34

JESS STOOD OUTSIDE THE DOOR marked VICTORIA LLEWELYN–STUDENT COUNSELING. Convinced the summons resulted from her disposing of Tim's sneakers, Jess considered saving everyone the trouble of her being formally expelled and just returning to her room and packing.

"Miss Lockhart?" A woman's voice flowed smoothly from the office.

Jess apologized and entered, taking a chair across from the desk.

The woman surprised Jess by taking a chair in front of the desk alongside her. Tentatively, they turned to face one another.

"How's it going?" the woman asked.

"Excellent."

"Are you nervous, Jessica?"

"A little, I guess," Jess lied. She was terrified.

"Because?"

"You know," Jess muttered.

"Tell me."

"Look, the only way I've managed to survive is by

sticking up for others." Jess's hands were sweaty; she tried to wipe them surreptitiously on her jeans. She couldn't meet Peggy's eyes.

"Commendable."

"If you don't understand— Wait? What?" Jess registered the woman's positive tone a little late.

"We encourage teamwork, Jessica. For many years, every executive position within the company had both a creative and a business side, each with its own employee. The system was modeled off the relationship between Walt and Roy. Teamwork leads to success in all avenues of life. Teamwork like that displayed by you and Amanda, for instance."

"Yeah, well, I guess."

"Before we continue, I must ask you to read this and, if you're agreeable, sign it." The woman pushed a sheaf of papers forward and smiled encouragingly. "It's a nondisclosure agreement. NDA, for short."

"I thought I signed everything already."

"You have signed a good many contracts, haven't you?" She had a warm smile; it seemed to stretch fully across her face. "In fact you signed a document very similar to this upon admittance. But this particular NDA is different. You must read it closely. It states that anything and everything said between us here today will never be spoken of again. Ever. It's to remain a secret, between us."

"That sounds ominous."

"Not at all. It just means we can talk openly and freely and that nothing said here gets repeated."

"Did Amanda sign one of these?"

"I couldn't tell you if she did, could I?" Another smile. "Let me ask you this: why do you think you're here? Why are we having this conversation?"

"If I don't help someone," Jess said tightly, looking back at her lap, "how can I expect anyone to help me?"

"Jessica, perhaps we should start over." Victoria "Peggy" Llewelyn gathered and composed herself.

"I'm not accusing her or you of anything."

"You aren't?"

"Why don't we start with the agreement. If you don't want to sign it, that's no problem. Meeting over. No harm done."

Meeting over? No dice; she wanted to know what was going on. Jess skimmed the document and signed. Peggy thanked her, and framed it deliberately into a stack of papers on her desk, careful to line up the corners with surgical precision.

"Jessica, our school seeks to foster accelerated development in certain individuals."

"No need to recruit me. I'm all in."

The woman's face was expressive as well as kind,

and she was given to pursing her lips to prevent a full smile and squinting to imitate amusement. It felt practiced. Oddly, she was nothing like the Peggy Amanda had described to Jess.

"That's what I want to talk to you about. Being 'all in.'" Her eyes never left Jess's as she spoke. "The Imagineers would like to invite you, Jessica, to join a group, an elite group of outstanding thinkers. It amounts to a think tank, but because we're Disney, we call it the Tink Tank."

Jess grinned. "Are you serious? I love it."

"The objective of the group is, paraphrasing Walt, 'To dream the future.'"

"Aha . . . my dreams."

"Your dreams. Yes."

"You aren't the first."

"I beg your pardon?"

"To want my dreams," Jess said, upset.

"Again, I believe you've misunderstood me, Jessica. No one wants to use you. We're familiar with your past, and we'd never repeat the trauma you and Amanda endured. We want to team you up with other extraordinary minds to explore opportunities in the present—and the future. Imagineers, DSI instructors, a few gifted personalities like yourself, all in the hope of bettering the company's future and, we hope, mankind's."

"Sounds lofty."

"And you sound bitter." Said with a purse of the lips.

"I'm used to it."

"A jump to a conclusion can be the last jump you ever take. Be careful, Jessica. I ask you only to think about it. To listen to what I'm saying and give it proper consideration.

"And remember: the Tink Tank and the offer to join it are to be kept secret *from everyone*, including other instructors, Imagineers, and your fellow students. That's the agreement you signed."

"You mean Amanda."

"That would include her. Yes. It's asking a lot, I know. But it's an imperative."

"I only talk to you about it."

"For now. Correct."

"I guess I don't actually understand what it is you're offering." Jess was finally meeting Peggy's eyes, striving to determine what she saw there.

"This is a big deal, Jessica. I'm not part of the Tink Tank, but I'm lucky enough to know about it, to be trusted to know about it, and to occasionally serve as a go-between."

"You're not a counselor. You're not even Victoria Llewelyn."

"I never introduced myself as such."

"The nameplate on the door says Victoria Llewelyn. That's not you."

"No."

"You're a lawyer."

"I am. I've borrowed this office for our meeting, as I don't typically work here at DSI."

"You work for the company."

"We all work for the company, dear."

"You tricked me."

"I never lied to you. Nor will I ever do so."

"You pretended—"

"Nothing. I made no pretense whatsoever. Had you asked, I would have gladly informed you of my name and position."

Jess studied her with heated eyes.

"Well, are you going to ask me?"

"No."

"I've upset you. Please accept my apology."

"Why didn't you just tell me who you were?" Jess said. To her dismay, her voice sounded whiny—weak.

"Until you signed the NDA, it wouldn't have been prudent. Once it was signed, you didn't ask, and the opportunity seemed to have passed."

"I don't like being lied to. I've been lied to my whole life."

"From what I've read, you've had an extraordinary life, one you have never allowed to break or destroy you. That resilience is part of why we're making you this offer."

"How many?"

"I beg your pardon?"

"How many of us are asked to join this thing?"

"Four," she answered.

There was silence. The words hung in the air between them. Jess's palms were sweating again, but for a different reason this time.

"Just four?"

"Yes. Four . . . in the past twelve years."

Jess couldn't speak.

"I don't imagine it's a terribly large group. Perhaps larger than six, fewer than ten. But I have no way of actually knowing. I just make the contracts."

"Between six and ten people," Jess's voice dropped to a whisper. "Out of everyone in the entire company."

"Correct."

"Me?"

"You." The unidentified woman nodded. Her expression implied envy. "You see? I'm afraid I have to remind you, any mention of anything said here may result in the filing of a lawsuit. And expulsion, of course."

"You'll sue me."

"The Tink Tank will take precautions to protect itself. The language is far stricter should you agree to join."

"More paperwork."

"Much."

"Me? Not Amanda?"

"Only you," the woman said. "As far as I know."

ANAHEIM, CALIFORNIA

A Different Disneyland

35

Amanda's e-mailed link to a folder containing the scanned documents from the basement vault launched the Keepers into action.

Even though it had been at Philby's request, Finn swelled with pride over how quickly Amanda had come through for them. She'd located, copied, and transmitted the IAV-471s in under twenty-four hours.

Because of her effort, Finn and Maybeck crossed over as DHIs into Disneyland's Central Plaza two nights later. Each carried a folder of printed pages sealed in a manila envelope, tucked into his back and covered by his shirt. DHI transmission of foreign objects on crossover was fairly reliable. The hope was that the files would cross over with Maybeck and Finn as holograms, and that splitting the folders into two would improve the chances of transmission.

What the boys were to do with this information once crossed over remained a mystery. The confusing instruction, "set to 1313," took Philby and Willa all of the first day and most of the second to figure out.

The key, they both agreed, was the verb, "set."

Philby decided the most obvious device that could be set to the number 1313 was an AM radio. However, Willa could find no online reference to a radio in Walt's apartment. Stymied, Finn e-mailed Becky Cline at the Walt Disney Archives and received a note back from Kevin Kern, one of the archivists charged with preserving historical items of Disney interest.

In the family apartment, it seemed, Walt kept a telephone, phonograph, and music box. No radio, Finn was told, though transistor radios had become popular in 1957, so a handheld set was not out of the question.

Just in case, Finn crossed over with his father's AM band Storm-Cast radio in his front pocket and Philby's jailbroken Return in his other. He and Maybeck made their way separately to Walt's apartment in Disneyland, meeting a few minutes past nine p.m., or twelve a.m. in Florida, where they slept.

Their first task was to remove the folders from the envelopes and inspect them. Sure enough, all but a few of the printed pages had crossed over intact—a major success. The radio proved to be a dud, however. KAZN, 1300 on the AM dial, was an Asian language station, and KWKW, 1330, was Spanish.

"Willa speaks Spanish," Maybeck said, looking at the set. "You should have crossed with her."

"We're fine," Finn said. "The backup plan is the gramophone and the music box. Philby said to check every square inch of both."

Finn inspected the gramophone. It had a control dial to adjust the speed, but no numbers beyond 78. The hand crank was just that, a crank, and he couldn't find any number 1313 on the needle head, serial number, or model number.

"Dude." The inflection Maybeck used when voicing the one-syllable appellation could convey disgust, irritation, snobbery, inquisitiveness, scorn, awe or, as was the case here, enthusiastic proclamation. He'd found something, and it obviously had to do with the standing lamp he held in his hand. Finn hurried over, kneeling beside Maybeck, facing the music box's side panel and its two controls.

One was a small lever: on/off. The other, an arcing metal band, allowed speed adjustment. The numbers corresponded to metronome settings, from 40 thru 208. *Grave* to *Prestissimo*.

"What am I missing?" Finn asked.

Maybeck waved the standing lamp across the side of the box. Light and shadows moved like a time lapse across the polished wood surface, dully reflecting back Maybeck and Finn's searching expressions from the polished wood.

"I've got nothing," Finn said.

Maybeck's long index finger tapped the far end of the curving scale, just past 208. "Look again." He moved the light more slowly.

A flash of brass-colored light caught Finn's eye, and he almost choked on his indrawn breath.

"Now you've got it!" Maybeck said.

Finn leaned in, rubbing DHI shoulders with Maybeck.

"How did you ever see this?"

"Artist's eye, dude." That particular use of *dude* was arrogance, but Finn didn't mind, because Maybeck had earned it. Carefully scratched into the metal with a pin or some kind of sharp tool, written not just by hand, but by the hand of an older man, was the number they'd been looking for.

1313

"'Set to 1313,'" Finn quoted. He didn't always feel his hologram heart's steady thumping, but he sure did now.

"Full throttle," Maybeck said. "There's no number past that one."

"So we set it to the max."

"Exactly."

"The carousel," Finn said, his voice the barest whisper. "Jingles."

"If Philby's right, you know what this means? We're going to time travel."

"We? You mean me."

"Oh, yeah. We," Maybeck said. "Giddy-up-go, Jingles. Yee-hah!"

"You *are* crazy."

"Yeah, well, before we start tripping through time, I'm going to write a little sonnet on your arm. Whatever we do, we've got to remember what got us here. There. Whatever."

"I wouldn't get my hopes up if I were you." Finn almost laughed at their role reversal, but spoke the words anyway, the words he'd heard so often over the last few days. Words he no longer believed because *he'd been there.* "There's no such thing as time travel."

"Says the kid with a pen drawn on one arm and a message on the other. You're afraid."

"Oh yeah," Finn said, his finger on the on/off switch, the speed set to 1313. "I'm terrified."

36

"**W**HAT THE—?" The inappropriate last word Maybeck used to end the sentence went unheard, thanks to rousing applause from a smattering of people. "Finn?"

"Yeah. Hang on," Finn said, inspecting his own black-and-white arms. "Okay. I've got this."

He clearly remembered being *inside* the television on the stage of Carousel of Progress. The fuzziness of his earlier attempt at memory was gone. It was as if the hypnotist had snapped his fingers, bringing Finn back—he remembered everything from his first ride on Jingles until now.

This picture tube felt even smaller, but basically the same. It was facing a busy Town Square, not a live audience. He also remembered the circus music playing on King Arthur Carrousel as he and Maybeck had arrived out of breath. The same music from Walt's apartment. He remembered people's faces trained up into the canopy of the carousel wondering about the sudden change in background music. He remembered timing his climbing onto the back of Jingles so that he and Maybeck arrived at the same instant.

Taking Maybeck by the arm, Finn turned him. "We're going to take three giant steps sideways, and jump. We'll land hard, so be ready for it. Follow my lead once we're out."

"Out?" Maybeck seemed paralyzed.

"Terry! Focus! Three steps. Shoulder to the glass."

"What glass?"

"Trust me." Finn pulled Maybeck back, stepping carefully. Then they spun to the side, and jumped through—and out!—of the television. Landing on and rolling across some asphalt, they got up and ran. They were full-size, though black-and-white.

Hordes of people milled around them, but none struck Finn as park guests. No, these were *workers*. Not Cast Members, but construction men. Even stranger, he didn't see a single female worker.

"This way!" Finn followed his instincts, leading Maybeck backstage near the firehouse. A moment later, they ducked beneath a fire escape, and Maybeck stopped to examine his black-and-white arms.

"Welcome to the world of two-dimensional DHIs," Finn whispered.

"Seriously old-school."

"I think we're looking for someone with a sign."

"What does the sign say? 'This way to insanity'?"

"Do you remember Jingles?"

"Who?"

"That's what I thought." Finn considered Maybeck's answer carefully. It seemed that his friend's memory had been wiped in crossing over. His had not. But this was not Finn's first journey.

He reached over and patted Maybeck's lower back. The hologram of his hand moved through the spot where the IAV documents should have been concealed; Finn touched his own back and made contact with the folder.

Apparently he and Maybeck had transitioned differently. Which meant that someone might be controlling the event.

Though a part of him resisted the logic of what he was seeing, it was only a small part. Finn understood, *this is the past.* Early Disneyland, early attractions, not the same park he knew. There were no guests. The construction workers wore dated clothing. They were dated people.

If he'd made this connection before, Finn didn't remember it. Maybe whoever had led them here and controlled their jump through time was protecting him from going bonkers, as he and Philby had discussed. Or perhaps whatever was happening was more unpredictable than the Keepers could imagine.

"I think he'll be looking for us," Finn said, sudden

understanding dawning. "The boy with the sign is here. Out there."

"I don't mean to be rude," Maybeck said, his voice uncharacteristically soft, "but I'd like to go home now."

Smiling stiffly, Finn whispered, "I hate to tell you this, Maybeck, but I think we're just getting started."

* * *

When they dared take another look into Town Square, they did so furtively.

"You know what this is?" Maybeck said in a belligerent tone that implied he knew he was wrong. "It's a film set. Talk about old-school! They must be setting up for a shot."

"Those aren't film cameras," Finn said, peering into Town Square from beneath the staircase. "You see how boxy they are? They're television cameras and monitors."

"A TV shoot?"

"Not *a* TV shoot," Finn said with emphasis, "*the* TV shoot. At the time, which I suppose is now, it was the largest live TV broadcast ever."

"No, no," Maybeck said. "I know this. The largest ever was . . . Wait a second! What the heck are you saying?" Only he didn't say *heck*. "Disney . . . land?"

"Isn't open yet. Opening day is going to be broadcast. More like Disney *lands*. Disney arrives on the scene."

Maybeck didn't seem to be breathing.

"Don't worry," Finn said. "When we go back, you won't remember any of this. Just like I didn't."

"What are you talking about?"

"Right! You don't remember that either!" Finn chuckled to himself. "This is awesome!"

Maybeck shook his head dismissively, studied his DHI again. "Come on, Finn. Is this some kind of prank? You and Philby messing with me?"

"More like the Imagineers messing with us. Walt's pen, Maybeck. It's all about Walt's pen." Finn showed him the faded drawing on his right forearm, and Maybeck's eyes widened.

"I remember that drawing."

"Good! Then whatever happens to our memories doesn't go that far back."

"The pen," Maybeck uttered reverentially.

"If we don't find Walt's pen, if we don't manage to get it so eventually it ends up in the One Man's Dream, then all this"—Finn gestured out at the bustling park, coming to life before their eyes—"comes crashing down. Whether it's the earthquake, the fire, or something else, the park will be destroyed, because we won't be able to stop the OTs."

"This can't be real," Maybeck muttered.

"Because we've never been part of strange stuff in the parks?" Finn said sarcastically.

"There's strange, and then there's this." Maybeck held up his black-and-white hand, and waggled it back and forth in Finn's face.

"Television!" Finn said. "The files we're carrying deal with the transmission of color television."

Maybeck's face lit up, then fell as he reached for the small of his back. "Mine are gone."

"Yeah, I know. I checked. We'll bring them next time."

"Next time? Seriously?"

"Completely."

"And this time?"

"We've got to find the guy with the sign," Finn said. "But if people see a couple of two-dimensional, black-and-white projections running around the park, they'll freak. The longer we stay hidden, the better."

"So why wasn't this guy waiting for you—*for us*—this time?"

"How do you know he wasn't?"

Maybeck crossed his arms. "Don't do that, man. That's spooky stuff."

"There was no Carousel of Progress on Opening Day," Finn said softly. Maybeck shook his head, confused.

"Meaning?"

"I think the first time I did this it was a test run. I'll explain later. If this guy was out there in Town Square, if he was watching for us, then he saw us head this way. I think you're onto something."

"I am?"

"Yeah. We wait. I think he'll come to us."

"Wait for how long?" Maybeck tried to keep his voice steady, but Finn could tell he was nervous.

"However long it takes," Finn said.

37

It took seven minutes. The boy in the cap had not shown up in Town Square, where the boys' attention was fixed, but in a folding lawn chair behind them. Finn practically jumped out of his holographic skin when he spotted him. He looked to be a year or two older than either Finn or Maybeck. He was dressed in work clothes that he'd owned for several years. His boots were scuffed and had leather soles, not rubber. Finn noticed this detail in particular. He had that every-man, common face.

"About-face," Finn whispered to Maybeck. They turned awkwardly, as one.

"Is that the boy?" Maybeck said out of the corner of his mouth.

"The same."

"Why's he just sitting there?"

"No clue."

"Why doesn't he say something?"

"No clue."

"Should we wave?"

Finn and Maybeck waved. The boy waved back.

"Well," Maybeck said. "This is creepy."

"Yup."

"Does he look familiar to you?" asked the artist, squinting critically at the boy's features.

"He looks like an extra from *Newsies*," Finn said, taking in the flat-topped cap, the suspenders holding up pants that stopped at the knee.

"Not his costume. Him."

"I don't think that's a costume."

"*Him!* Look at his face, you idiot!"

"Maybe a little," Finn admitted, looking more closely. The boy was staring at them, amused. He hadn't moved.

"More than a little. Did we see him in a photo or something? Maybe in Walt's apartment?"

"Could be. I suppose we could ask."

Now the boy in the chair motioned for them to come to him, a smile breaking out across his face.

Maybeck spoke so softly Finn had to guess at his words. "We're DHIs. He can't hurt us. Right?" He didn't sound convinced.

"Not exactly," Finn said. "Stuff can hurt, so be careful."

"Okay, got it." Maybeck stepped away from the concealing wall and, with Finn following him stride for stride, walked up to the boy, who remained seated, legs crossed at the ankle, fingers steepled together.

"Howdy," the guy said.

Finn didn't answer. He leaned forward and slipped the folder into the boy's hands. "The other one didn't cross over."

"Transmit?"

"We call it 'crossing over.'"

"No fooling? And who do you mean when you say 'we'?"

"The five of us."

"Five? I only see two. Where are the rest?"

"They're hiding," Maybeck said.

With his head buried as he examined the papers Finn had delivered, the boy spoke. "Holy smokes! This is fab!" Finn understood the comment was meant for him.

"I'm glad," Finn said.

"I'm just curious. Where'd you get the keen rags?"

"Our clothes?" Maybeck said. But Finn shook his head slightly to shut Maybeck up.

"Costume shop. Tomorrowland," Finn said.

"Makes sense, I guess. So you broadcast from over there?"

Finn realized this guy didn't know much, maybe even knew less than him and Maybeck. He tried to sort it out.

"You drew on my arm, right?"

The guy had no clue, and was not embarrassed to show it.

Finn decided to put the facts out there. "We brought you the file. So, can you please tell us what's going on?"

"Are you who wrote me?" the guy asked.

"Maybe you've got the wrong boys and we've got the wrong guy."

"Will someone tell me what's going on?" Maybeck sounded ready to hurt this kid.

"What do you think is going on?" the boy asked.

"By the look of it, the cameras and all, it's 1955," Finn said.

"Why wouldn't it be?"

Finn and Maybeck exchanged a look. Ahead of them, the boy continued flipping pages, his eyes scanning rapidly through the folder.

"The cameras," Maybeck said. "The TV thing. Opening Day. It's almost Disneyland Opening Day."

"Heck, yes!" the boy said, and smiled again. He had a warm face, clear and welcoming.

"July?"

"The fourteenth. The fog kept it cool this morning, but it'll be a real scorcher later."

"Thirteen thirteen. The code for the music box. It sent us here, to this day."

"I don't know what you're saying, boy. Don't know what you're talking about."

"That makes three of us," Maybeck said.

The kid closed the file. "What other papers?"

"There's more."

"Over in Tomorrowland?"

"Not exactly," Finn said.

"Pretty close, actually," Maybeck said.

"I can bring them," Finn offered. "Maybe tonight."

"No!" delivered sharply by a boy with nervous eyes. "I need time. Rome wasn't built in a day. Give me two days. Can you do that? The seventeenth of July. Understand? That's when we—you—can begin the real work."

"The real work?" Maybeck asked.

For the first time, the boy looked concerned. His brow wrinkled, and his gaze moved from Finn to Maybeck, then back.

"Listen, boys, this is new to me. It's a bona fide gas, but my noggin's a little fuzzy."

"What does that mean?" Maybeck said, sounding alarmed.

"Your name?"

"Maybeck."

"Like the architect, Bernard Maybeck! Impressive." He considered Maybeck for a long time. He looked at

Finn. "I don't want to frighten you boys. It's important you not be frightened. Maybe tell your friends to come out of hiding."

"Not now," Maybeck said. "Maybe later."

"Ditch the costumes next time. No need to look ridiculous."

"Next time," Finn muttered, shaking his head, trying to keep himself calm; trying to keep himself all clear. "I think," he whispered to Maybeck, "this is the guy who draws the pen on my arm. But not for a few more years."

Maybeck looked at Finn like Finn had lost it completely.

"You brought us here," Maybeck said to the kid. "You must know something."

"Just following what I was told," the boy said.

"Two days," Finn proposed.

"Copacetic! You understand?" the boy said, raising an eyebrow.

"Maybe not," Maybeck said. Finn put a hand on his arm, cutting him off.

"Yeah, we do. I will bring you the other folder in two days."

"'Days are nights. Nights are days.' You wrote that."

"We didn't write anything!" Maybeck complained.

"You'll be waiting for us."

The guy hoisted the folder. "I should be, all things considered."

Finn found himself amused. "We'll be here. At least four. Hopefully all five."

"That's good leadership, Finn."

Finn winced at use of his name. A name he'd not provided. He put a hand to his DHI forehead, whispered, "Oh my gosh!" under his breath. He felt his consciousness swoon. He'd been hit, hurt and worse, while a DHI, but he'd never fainted.

He fought the sensation, telling himself that he couldn't experience a loss of blood pressure if he didn't have blood. The feeling grew clearer: he wasn't passing out, he was freezing up, like a computer crashing.

"... eeh ... ne ... ou ... hu ... uuu ... re." If that was his voice he was hearing, it was emerging at half speed. He sounded like a comedian pretending to be drunk. He tried again. "... ehh ... no ..." A complete meltdown. He was looking *up* at Maybeck; he was lying down, his body prone. Sparkles filled the space around Maybeck's face, flitting about like a swarm of fireflies.

Maybeck's giant black-and-white face was leaning over him. Finn sat up. Maybeck offered him a hand.

"That was not supposed to happen," the boy said, studying Finn like he was a specimen under a microscope.

"That was so cool, dude," Maybeck whispered. "You scattered like dust and then reassembled. Awesome effect."

Finn barely heard him. All his attention was directed at the boy in the cap; to the lines of his face. "I know who you are!" His voice was a whispered shout, a dying cry. "I know you!"

The kid's blue eyes sparkled with mirth. He allowed himself a gentle, familiar smile. He laughed.

38

FINN AND MAYBECK RETURNED as a pair onto the rump of Jingles, just behind a young boy dressed as Woody. Breathless, Finn pulled Maybeck off the horse and, amid shouting from the ride operator, off the carousel itself.

As they ran, Finn marveled at how, this time, he remembered everything. He knew they'd been in Disneyland of old; he knew the date they'd been there, the weather; that a television crew had been setting up for the historic opening of the park. He knew who had arranged it all, too, but he had yet to allow the name to leave his lips. It filled the hollow spot in his chest, though; it swelled with warmth and happiness and excitement. He felt teased by possibility. He wanted to jump back onto Jingles and take another ride.

"What the hey?" Maybeck said. "Why'd you pull me off like that?"

Finn, about to rip him, recalled his own first ride on Jingles and softened. Still, he rushed his words. "I know you don't remember anything, Maybeck, but you gotta trust me. We have to get to Central Plaza. We're gonna return." He and Maybeck were three-dimensional, full-color holograms once more, to Finn's delight. "Stay all clear," he added. "Version 1.6, remember? We can't afford fear."

"Got it."

"Are you sure? Can you rise above it?"

"It's Disneyland, man. Check it out."

Finn did. The lights were bright and high, the sounds of traffic pronounced. The guests wore normal clothes. It was night, not day, as it had been in the other Disneyland. Men and women—there were women everywhere—carried smartphones, and the only hats the men wore were baseball caps. A child slurped loudly on a plastic straw in a disposable cup, and Finn blinked, realizing he hadn't seen a single piece of plastic on "the other side" (as he was now thinking of it).

Maybeck was still looking too relaxed. The hazards of forgetting everything.

"You remember what Willa told us about Mr. Toad?" Finn said pointedly.

"Yeah, there is that. I hear you, man."

"Good," Finn said, glad that Maybeck could recall the recent past on this side. "If we're seen in the parks, the Imagineers are going to freak. They'll ground us. We have to reach the plaza as quickly as possible! Keep your eyes peeled. We stay in crowds, hang close with our heads down. And we move fast."

"Aye, aye."

"I'm serious."

"I can tell."

To their left a group of five life-size playing cards materialized—four Jacks and a Queen. They were from the Mad Tea Party attraction. They turned to face the boys and, as they did, a crowd immediately formed as if this was a street show.

"Bad news," Finn said, sticking his arm out to stop Maybeck as he put on the brakes. "If they're interested in us, they're OTs."

"It's worse than you think," Maybeck said. "How much do you know about Jacks?"

"Zero."

"I studied this stuff in a figure drawing class, and if these boys are from a French card deck, we're in trouble. The four Jacks represented Europe's greatest warriors, knights like Lancelot and the dude from the *Iliad*."

"I hated that book."

"Whatever. Hector was willing to die for anything he deemed right."

"They're armed. They want to kill us." Finn's voice was flat, certain.

"Or die trying," said Maybeck. "You recognize the fifth."

"Is that—?"

"The Queen of Hearts. Who, in my opinion, is just plain deranged."

Behind the boys another line of cards arrived, mostly clubs and spades with lower numbers.

"What can *they* do?" Finn asked, pointing them out to Maybeck, who hadn't seen them, his attention absorbed by the royal suits ahead.

"Dude." It came out: *Doooood.* Finn didn't hear that tone from Maybeck often. It meant he didn't like what he saw. It meant he was *scared.* "How can the OTs be back?"

"Don't allow the fear!" Finn said. "Do not let them pull you out of all clear."

"No one has to do that, man. I did it all by myself."

"Recover."

"As if. The OTs are dead!"

APPARENTLY NOT, Finn wanted to scream. "I don't think they're organized. They're like terrorists with no leader." He hoped to sound bold and brave, but he knew the truth: he'd lost some of his all clear as well. This round to the cards, to their slow, ominous show of force. "I suppose," he said, swiveling from front to back, trying to keep the enemy in full sight, "that the clubs can club us. And spades are shovels, so that's not good, either."

"Don't look now, but they're forming a card house," Maybeck muttered uncomfortably. "They look pretty organized to me!"

On all sides, park guests stepped out of the way, enthralled with the cards' lockstep movements, which were reminiscent of a marching band formation. The cards lined up, edge-to-edge and edge-to-face, in an octagon shape, the circumference of which was ever shrinking.

"They're boxing us in," Maybeck said, spinning one way, then another.

"Duh! I got that."

"Any ideas, Einstein?"

Making the boys' situation all the more dangerous, the cards morphed into three dimensions, horses growing forward out of the four Jacks, their hooves impacting hard on the ground. It looked as if the giant cards had cut the horses in half, leaving only the front of their bodies. Next, the Jacks' arms lifted up and off the face of the cards. One held a mace, another a sword, a third a battle-ax, and the last a halberd. The crowd went wild.

"Slice and dice," Maybeck groaned.

The guests cleared a wide space around the boys; they seemed to be expecting a show. When Maybeck or

Finn tried to take so much as a step forward, the cards closed the gap. The boys were penned in on all sides, surrounded by a crazed Queen, four weapon-wielding warriors, and four additional six-foot-tall cards with three-dimensional clubs and spades waving.

"We're about to get hammered."

Finn barely heard Maybeck's joke, his focus on how to survive in the face of such odds. "If we can all clear," he whispered, the cards' edges sliding on the card faces before them, the octagon shrinking, collapsing inward, "we can walk right through them."

"And if we could fly, we could fly over them, *Peter*." Maybeck spun in a full circle, desperate. "I'm so far from all clear that I might as well not be a hologram."

"Yeah. What about going under them?"

"Hey, I missed that," Maybeck said, and there was sudden hope in his voice.

The cards stood on their corners, raised up on a fold of paper that functioned as an ankle. The process of lifting bent the card slightly, creating a small gap beneath the bottom edge and the asphalt.

"We're thicker than that, though," Maybeck said.

"We'll never budge a horse, but the others . . ." Finn spun to face the spades and clubs. Nines and tens mostly. Clubs flailing. Spades swinging.

"We'll get beaten to high heaven," Maybeck said.

The space narrowed again. If they didn't do *something*, the boys were going to suffer.

"No, look! There's a pattern. Ten of clubs!" The spiky weapons struck out from the face of the card in two columns of four and a middle column of two. The top five lifted and fell in unison, their motion opposite that of the bottom five, which also rose and fell as one.

"Got it!" Maybeck said. "We go on the next lift."

As the top five clubs lowered, the bottom group rose. The boys dove. Maybeck, who was taller, arrived first, thrusting his arm through the gap beneath the card. The card moved, but proved too heavy for a partial hologram.

An instant later, Finn joined him, thrusting up with both arms. He slid his knees under him, and lifted with the full strength of his back. Together, he and Maybeck threw the card into the air.

As it rose, the boys rolled, came to their feet and—

—ran smack into a thick crowd of park guests.

The cards were not pleased. They pivoted, producing a strong wind that swept hats off heads and sent stuff flying in all directions, and *ran* for the two boys. A spade caught Finn on the shoulder and dropped him to the pavement. Another smacked his head. Maybeck called out in pain as two clubs hammered his arms and shoulders with blows.

The crowd cheered. As he struggled to sort out why any group would celebrate violence being done to a pair of boys, the spades rained down upon him. Shoulder. Forearm. Several blows to the head. He was losing consciousness.

"Not . . . good . . ." he mumbled, having no idea if Maybeck could hear him.

His vision blurry, Finn looked up and saw another spade, aiming directly at the top of his head. He knew he wouldn't survive, not with his all clear spent, his body solid. He reflected on how many such battles he'd made it through in the past, how lucky he'd been, how he and his friends had been so sure the Overtakers were done, broken. Finished.

They were wrong. At the very moment in which he and Maybeck had accomplished something fantastic and impossible—it was all about to end. And all before he could explore the new realm—the realm of the past.

If he were to die anywhere, Finn thought, watching the spade descend upon him, then Disneyland or the Magic Kingdom was the most fitting of places. He braced himself for the final blow.

39

I<small>T STRUCK LIKE A GUST OF WIND.</small> Not wind generated by the cards. A ferocious gale-force blow, the kind that topples a beach house caught by the leading edge of a hurricane.

Yet, it wasn't wind. It was a force, like magnetism or gravity. The cards lifted like kites, flying horses, swinging clubs, and all. They crashed onto the roof of Mr. Toad's Wild Ride, the crowd erupting at the sight in shouts, whistles, and cheers.

Finn skidded across the asphalt, caught up as inexorably as the cards. If he hadn't been a partial hologram, his pants might have shredded at the knees. Oddly, his hair never waved; his shirt never ruffled. So if it wasn't wind, what was it? he wondered.

Maybeck, still standing, skated the same distance as Finn. The crowd parted, not impeding their travel. Finn spun around into the direction of the dying wind, and he saw her. His earlier text, suggesting they might have a moment to meet, hadn't been ignored. He had not expected it to be like this.

A girl. A girl that made his chest tight and his voice catch. She stood out from the crowd, a few kids just behind her fading from Finn's vision as if they were nothing.

"Amanda?" That was Maybeck.

It was Amanda—and Jess. And beside them, a tall kid with crazy black hair.

"Look out!" the tall boy shouted.

Two of the horses and their cards jumped from the roof and landed effortlessly on the ground. The Jack of Hearts raised his sword, drawing it back over his shoulder.

But as he raked his arm forward, preparing to cleave Maybeck's head in half, the sword stayed behind. His chain mail glove swung down, empty-handed. The sword, its sharpened tip pointing toward the sky, floated off the horse and stopped some four feet from the ground.

"Knaves!" the Jack of Hearts cried, his horse rearing up and neighing. "My sword is possessed! Cursed! These lads are of the black magic. It's the work of the Magi." He pointed to Maybeck. "You will die, sorcerer! But another day!"

He continued to back away; the other cards slipped off the roof and gathered about him. As one, they turned and ran; the Jacks rode, the Queen of Hearts trailed.

Once they were a safe distance away, she waved her scepter in a broad sweep. She led the other cards in the direction of their attraction. As they ran, they dissolved, like ash.

The air seemed to move; some people in the crowd lost their balance, as if they'd been shoved aside. The Jack's sword flew toward Finn and clanked to the pavement at the last second, skidding within inches of his feet.

Thunderous applause sounded. Amanda rushed to Finn and Maybeck, apologizing as she ran. "I'm so sorry!"

"Sorry?" Maybeck said incredulously.

"You *saved* us," Finn said, throwing his hologram arms around her. He squeezed, but his hologram arms passed through her body—he'd returned to all clear. Jess and the tall boy laughed. The crowd oohed.

Focusing on making his hands solid, Finn bent and hoisted the sword, the gesture driven by curiosity, not triumph. The crowd misunderstood and cheered loudly.

"Did you see that . . ." he asked Amanda, ". . . *ghost?*"

"Ah, yeah. Actually, that's Emily, a friend of mine," Amanda said. "You're going to like her."

40

"So you're saying you saw all this, but Terry didn't?"

Connected by video on Willa's tablet, Charlene's voice was clear, even though her image was not. She'd just come from a shoot for her television show, meaning her hair was perfect, her makeup was perfect; she was perfect. But her perfect voice expressed only cynical disbelief as she said, "And why is that?"

The four other Keepers sat on the kitchen countertops in Maybeck's Aunt Bess's house, competing for space with pieces of pottery in all stages of completion. The kitchen cabinets' glass fronts offered a view to even more artistic mugs, plates, bowls, and cups in a rainbow of colors and an assortment of shapes.

On the counter, the kids nibbled oatmeal cookies that Bess had baked specially for them. Like Mrs. Whitman, Bess supported the Keepers and believed in their cause.

Finn, bruised and sore from the battle with the cards, kicked his legs back against the cabinet behind him and sighed. The Keepers had ambushed him. He'd gone to Maybeck's to collect the second folder, only to find Willa and Philby there as well—along with the video connection to Charlene in Los Angeles. Philby wouldn't agree to cross Finn back into Disneyland without a full explanation and group consensus. At the moment, it wasn't going terribly well. Finn had withheld the most important piece of information, fearing he might hit the resistance he was now encountering.

"Remember," Finn said to Philby, "Mom telling us about people who claimed to have time traveled, that they ended up in loony bins? First of all, that's how you're treating me." He spoke now to them all. "Second, to answer your question, Charlie, what if memory, my ability to retain events, is being controlled by whoever made this happen?"

"Finn's onto something, you guys," Maybeck said. "I remember nothing about what happened. Zero. Zilch. I climbed onto Jingles, and then Finn was pulling me off."

"So?" Charlene again, on the tablet. "Maybe that's all there was to it!"

"No. Think for a sec! That's exactly what happened to Finn the first time he crossed over. Right? He remembered nothing."

"I love you, Finn. You know that!" Charlene said argumentatively. "Seriously, I want to believe you traveled back in time to a couple days before Disneyland officially opened. I mean, who *wouldn't* want to believe that? But do you know how deranged this sounds? Black-and-white? Jumping out of a television and then back in? The next thing you know, you'll be telling us you met Wayne and Walt and took a tour of the park before it opened."

"Not that last part," Finn said.

The three faces in the kitchen turned in his direction.

"Now this is getting interesting," Philby said.

"There was a guy our age," Finn said. "Wearing one of those flat caps, like in *Newsies*. He was spying on me and Maybeck. Didn't seem the least bit weirded out by a pair of black-and-white two-dimensional projections trying to hide beneath the staircase to Walt's apartment."

Finn hadn't just waded into the water. He'd dived in. But he figured it was too late to ease into the truth. Better to make a splash. "He waved us over to him and we went." He paused, looked at his friends' faces. Philby: excited interest. Willa: skeptical fascination. Maybeck: confusion. But Charlene didn't so much as twitch. Maybe the screen had frozen. "He asked me— not Terry, me—for the IAV file. He expected me to have it. I handed it over, explaining that Terry's half hadn't projected properly. He didn't seem to question that explanation, which made me realize he must be the guy who'd done this. Once we'd returned, Terry and me, I thought about it some more. You know what's in those files? Philby?"

Philby's voice was hushed and reverential. "The first folder was the schematics for the shadow mask cathode ray tube *color* television. But the second folder involves—get this!—white-light transmission holography, a technology developed by Polaroid in the late nineteen sixties." He paused. "Combined, they're the ingredients for—"

"Color holograms!" Willa blurted out. "Finn brought this guy the schematics to project DHIs," Willa said.

"One can't have black-and-white, two-dimensional projections trying to find Walt's pen and putting it back where it belongs."

"You see?" Finn pleaded. "You see how it fits together and makes sense?"

"No," Charlene said. So the tablet hadn't frozen after all, Finn thought wryly. "I don't want to be the jerk here, and I think that's what I'm being, and I'm so sorry, you guys."

"I was the one there, and I don't fully believe it," Finn said. "You have every right to doubt, Charlie."

"The thing is," Willa said, "it does make sense. It adds up. Holography was theorized in 1947 by a scientist working with microscopes. What held up its full development was . . . any guesses? . . . the lack of *color* light waves and multisource projection imaging. Single source, single color light didn't work."

"Let me guess," Philby said. "All it gave you was two-dimensional, black-and-white projections?"

"Dude," Maybeck said. His whispered exclamation loosely translated as: *I can't believe what I'm hearing.*

Finn cleared his throat. "I was expected there because I was talking to the guy who'd written the thirteen-thirteen clue on my arm. A *much younger* version of the same guy, a guy basically our age, maybe twenty or twenty-one. A guy who, at that time, was unaware he'd already met me, a bunch of years later, in the Carousel of Progress, or that he'd drawn a pen on my arm."

He paused, allowing it to sink in. Of the faces focused on him, only Philby was already smiling. Only Philby knew where this was headed.

Finn took a deep breath, lifted his chin slightly, and stated unequivocally: "I was talking to Wayne Kresky."

41

Jess sat with several adults around a long conference table in a windowless room. The door was both closed and locked.

To her left was a well-known Disneyland art designer. To her right, a guy in his late twenties in jeans and trendy glasses; he looked like a young Bono, from U2. Jess thought she recognized others—maybe the pioneer computer guy whose name she couldn't remember. Another looked an awful lot like a famous film director. Those gathered either worked for the company or served on its board. The woman pretending to be Peggy had made it clear the Tink Tank was not for outsiders.

Jess had been invited to the meeting by a text sent anonymously:

Tink Tank, Building 2, #208, 3PM

The meeting was chaired by a woman in her forties. She spoke confidently and warmly. No names were used. Nor was there mention of Jess's addition to the group. Jess caught herself clenching her hands tightly to remind herself this was actually happening. She was sitting here with famous people, the newest member of a secret think tank.

What?!!

"We have a serious development to discuss that's not on the agenda. Consider it new business," the chairwoman said. "Compelling video evidence shows that two of our original DHIs were recently in the park in an unauthorized capacity. Even more troublingly, additional evidence appears to support the idea that the insurgents have returned in an organized capacity." She paused. Jess kept all expression off her face as she watched the others at the table; they showed deep concern. But to their credit, no one gasped or tried to add drama to the situation.

"Insurgents," Jess said, "as in Overtakers?"

The chairwoman chose not to respond. "I would like to address the task of discipline and, perhaps more importantly, what if anything we can do to round up and subordinate the insurgents."

A hand went up. "Does this have anything to do with the unauthorized activity in Walt's apartment?" he asked.

"Everything," the chairperson answered. "The two problems appear to be one and the same."

Jess felt sick to her stomach: they knew everything!

Was that why she was here? Were they going to try to use her to spy on her friends?

"Young lady?" It took Jess a moment to realize she was the one being addressed. She nodded. "Is there now, or has there ever been, anything in your dreams to suggest the recurrence of this . . . unrest?"

There it was, out on the table: *in your dreams.* Yet, no one seemed surprised to hear the chairwoman's words. Only then did it occur to Jess that these people had likely voted on her joining the Tink Tank.

She knew better than to lie. Somehow, she was certain that everything spoken in this room would be the truth and would be kept secret forever. "No, ma'am." She wasn't sure what to call the woman. "My darkest dreams—that's what I call them—have been about Ursula, Maleficent, and my friends. The original DHIs you're talking about. I know them. Very well."

"And what are they up to?" Another woman, the art director. "How are they able to do what they're doing?"

"Wayne . . . Wayne Kresky left a message, a code that led them to Walt's apartment."

"The music box," the computer guy said. "Tesla's music box."

"Who?" Jess asked.

"Nikola Tesla. A turn-of-the-century electronic genius responsible for the building blocks of much of the electrical engineering we use today. An inventory of Walt and Lillian's house goods in 1968 revealed the initials 'NT' on the back of Walt's music box. But the link has stymied the Imagineers for decades."

"That fits," Jess said, nodding.

"With?" The art director quirked an eyebrow at her.

"Recent events. Not my dreams. Not exactly. But it fits. Can I tell you guys something?" Jess said, realizing too late that this was the point of a think tank. No one answered, so she continued. "Two nights ago, the event you're talking about with the DHIs and the Overtakers . . . My sister was there. Amanda. She battled the cards with telekinesis. Finn had returned as a DHI with Maybeck. Terry Maybeck."

"Returned from?" the computer guy again.

"It's a term they use."

"I'm aware of the term."

"Of course. Well, get this!" she said excitedly. "First, he crosses over from Orlando to Walt's apartment. Philby does that. But then, he gets on the carousel and his DHI vanishes. It's like a double crossover. Like *Inception*. A different layer."

"I'm familiar with the film and the concept," said the guy she now knew *was* the famous director.

"It has something to do with color television transmission. Philby asked for files on that."

Several at the table took notes.

"This is all between us?" Jess asked. "Stays between us."

"Absolutely!" said the chairwoman.

"It has something to do with Walt's pen. With the first time the Keepers saved the Magic Kingdom."

Baffled glances passed around the table.

"Can you explain that?" the computer guy said.

"It, the pen, redrew the Magic Kingdom during the first big defeat of the OTs. Without that redraw, the Magic Kingdom would have fallen. And where would we be now if that had happened? Not here, that's for sure! You talk about evidence," this to the chairperson. "Well, Wayne showed the Keepers—the original DHIs—that there's a disconnect. In several photographs, and in one of my dreams, Walt's pen isn't where it needs to be if it's to show up in One Man's Dream. And if it isn't there when the Keepers go looking for it . . . You see? So, something changed. Something, someone, had to have put the pen into the mug on Walt's desk in the first place."

"That's a lot to process," said the film director.

"I know. But the bottom line is, the DHIs, the Keepers, have to get that pen back where it belongs."

"What exactly are they attempting to do?" asked a quiet woman sitting next to the art director.

The art director interrupted. Her words were spoken as if she feared the answer. "What are the chances that what we're hearing now has to do with the oil? The observations?"

Jess blinked, suddenly confused. The chairperson noticed and spoke kindly to her.

"You have been given your user name and password. I suggest you read the minutes of the past six—no, seven—meetings as soon as possible. Immediately, actually. Report back to me when you've completed that assignment."

"Of course."

"I see where you're going with this." The computer man was staring hard at the art director; he'd seemingly blocked out everyone else at the table. "Tesla. Wayne Kresky. Kids disappearing from the carousel. The *events*. What you're calling the oil."

"Is it even possible?" the art director asked, and then repeated softly, "Is such a thing possible?"

"One of the points you will read about," the chairperson said to Jess, "is a series of disturbances within certain attractions, a quality to the air, what we call 'oil.' It's required us to shut down those attractions on many occasions, claiming refurbishment. We've had to work hard to ascertain that the attractions are still safe for our guests."

Jess nodded, trying to process, to put it all together. "I need access to the basement archives in the Tower. The dorm," she said.

Heads turned; the attendees' eyes met, silently checking with one another. In the end, the chairperson spoke for them.

"You know about the incident? That was you?"

"Not me. But yes, I know about it."

Some more quick eye conversations took place.

"I'm not going to rat them out, so don't even ask."

"Fine. Given your compliance with the secrecy clause, I don't see a problem in providing you access. But only you. No friends. No discussion. And you will supply us with a full accounting of what it is you're after, why, and what you find. We'll find an archivist to assist you."

"Sounds good," Jess said.

"What else do you know about all this?" The quiet woman sounded accusatory.

"Nothing leaves this room, is that right? Or are some of you allowed to share what we talk about with others?"

"We only share with one another," the chairwoman said firmly. "Mind you, actions may be taken as a result of that sharing. The point of the Tink Tank is to envision a future for the company. That includes making the present a safe and agreeable place, one that will allow the best creativity to flourish."

"Look," Jess said, "I don't know how any of this works, but I do know that if Walt's pen can't be found in One Man's Dream, then everything the Kingdom Keepers—the DHIs—have done for the company . . . well, it never happens. Right? They *found the pen*, and they saved the Magic Kingdom, so obviously it gets there somehow. But when you study archival photographs—and when I dreamed it—the pen wasn't, isn't, there. Something changes that." She paused, remembering. "Wayne left them a message, too. 'It's about time.'"

The quiet woman gasped. The computer guy looked at Jess with an intensity that made her turn instinctively away.

"We've already talked about this," Jess said, trying to keep her voice steady. "I realize that. I'm not trying to waste anyone's time. But the point is, at least *I think* the point is, that something's going on with them—Finn and the Keepers—that has to do with time, with the carousel. It has to do with the Overtakers, too. They aren't dead. They're back. But honestly, I don't know anything about that. Not really."

"It's intriguing," the computer man said. "Well worth sharing. I think I can speak for all of us in thanking you."

Around the table, heads nodded.

"But when you say the 'original DHIs,'" Jess said, "what exactly does that mean?" She faced the chairperson, who seemed to deliberate carefully before answering.

"There are six new version 2.8 DHIs in development."

"Two-point-eight?!"

"They're something special," the computer guy said. He looked like he was holding back an impulsive grin.

"And the originals? What happens to them?"

"No need for us to dwell on that now," said the chairwoman briskly.

"What . . . happens . . . to . . . them?" Jess said, her demanding tone unmistakable.

"They will be decommissioned, of course." The chairwoman gave a brief, exasperated sigh. "When Mickey or Minnie, when any of our characters receives a refresh, the originals are sent to the Archives for safe-keeping. Becky is a member of our little group." She nodded at a small woman in spectacles toward the end of the table. "It's all handled with kid gloves, I assure you."

Decommissioned. The word echoed inside Jess's head. *Archives? Sworn to secrecy!* That meant she couldn't tell the Keepers; couldn't alert them.

She started to speak but was cut off.

"Is there a way to shut down the DHIs for now?" The film director addressed this question to the entire group.

The computer man answered. "If they're projecting without the cooperation of the Imagineers, they've gained access through a back door or a hack. Finding it could take time. The easiest way would be to shut down the projectors themselves."

Jess felt like she had an ice cube stuck in her throat. These people were, for the sake of the company, going to shut down the Keepers. Her friends. They were going to stop them just as they reached the heart of the mystery.

"I believe it's best for the safety of all concerned," said a woman who hadn't spoken until then.

"Though as we all know, the same projectors are used for the version 2.0 guides currently in the park. They're wildly popular and a strong source of revenue." The computer man made it obvious he thought his own suggestion had its drawbacks.

The art director spoke next. "What if we find out when the DHI hosts are most popular? We could then shut down the projection system entirely for the remainder of the time."

"That's the first good idea I've heard," said the man

with trendy glasses. Jess felt a rush realizing he looked as much like Bono as Bono. "Is that doable?"

"Filters?" the art director asked. "Is there any way we can screen the earlier versions, but allow the current ones?"

"Not really," Mr. Computer said. "Two-point-oh is a build out of 1.6, so it's not an option." He turned to the chairwoman. "Let's try Connie's suggestion. Full shutdown, limiting 2.0 to only its most popular hours."

"I remind *everyone*," the chairwoman spoke directly to Jess, "that we've sworn and signed an oath." She seemed to be reacting to the man's use of a proper name, but Jess would find out later that that was how the chairwoman closed every meeting. On this first day, Jess took it in a deeply personal way.

Heads nodded.

Jess nodded too, though inside she felt light-headed and dry-mouthed.

Decommissioned.

ANAHEIM, CALIFORNIA

Anaheim Ducks Arena

42

THE SIZE OF THE INDOOR ARENA, the noise level and excitement before the hockey game even got started, vibrated up through one's feet and into one's bones like a passing subway train. The air was chilly and smelled of popcorn and hot dogs. About half the seats were occupied; many spectators wore jerseys displaying unpronounceable names with more consonants than vowels. Vendors in yellow neon vests shouted out "Beer!" and "Cotton candy!"

Players for the Anaheim Ducks and the St. Louis Blues skated by, passing in a blur around the ice in pregame warm-up mode. Searchlights swept the rink, throwing starlike shadows off each player. The overhead scoreboard flashed with colorful advertisements and messages to fans: GET READY TO MAKE SOME NOISE!

Tim made a point of having Jess go down Row HH first. He went behind her, followed by Amanda. Jess waited for men to stand and women to tuck their legs out of the way as she inched along. She found the proper seat and plunked down.

"Wow!" she said.

"Yeah, I know," Tim said, smiling at her.

"You shouldn't have treated us," Jess said. "Must have cost a fortune."

"Mr. Dry gave us his four season tickets. He couldn't use them tonight."

"*The* Mr. Dry? Assistant head of school?"

"How many do you know?"

"Four?" Amanda said, overhearing and leaning across Tim in a way Jess didn't appreciate. "Mr. and Mrs. and two kids. But there are only three of—"

"Jess, Amanda, meet Nick Perkins." Tim motioned to the boy sitting next to Jess. Younger by several years, judging by his size, he showed little emotion, his eyes and facial expression both carefully controlled.

"—us." Amanda said hello, followed by Jess.

Nick nodded faintly. He seemed more interested in what was happening on the ice than in making two new friends.

"He can be shy," Tim whispered into Jess's ear.

"Do I look like I care?" she whispered back.

"You care. Believe me, you care. You thought I brought you here to see ice hockey? I hate ice hockey! I'm a lacrosse guy any day."

Jess turned to face the boy to her left. "Tim tells me I should speak to you. He says you're shy, but I don't believe it."

"He says you and Amanda are the real deal."

"Whatever that means."

"Disneyphiles."

"Well, that part's true."

"You know the Kingdom Keepers." Nick paused. "Tim says you can get a message to them."

"Did he?" Jess realized the boy was either older than he looked or exceptionally smart. Maybe both. What had Tim gotten her into? "I suppose anything's possible," she said, not wanting to confirm her friendship with the group. For their sakes, not hers.

"I'm the rumor guy," Nick said.

"Is that right?"

"BigEars-dot-biz."

"That's you?"

"And my four employees."

"Employees? Seriously?"

"W-2s and all. We do a little bit better and I'll have to provide health insurance."

How about babysitting? Jess wondered. Even if she gave him a few extra years, he couldn't yet be fourteen.

"I've never been big on rumors," she said.

"There are plenty about you and Amanda."

"I'll bet there are."

"And the Kingdom Keeper ships. Like Fimanda.

Charbeck. That Willa and Philby . . . well, that they argue a lot."

"That's putting it mildly. They're both too smart." Jess chuckled.

"Apparently Mr. Toad's Wild Ride was shut down because of them."

"Makes a good rumor, doesn't it? Listen, if you're going paparazzi on my friends, I am so out of here." Jess spun to her right and hissed, "What were you thinking, Tim?"

As she stood, a hand on her shirt tugged her back down. It was Nick. "Hey!" she punched him. Hard. "You do not touch me or my clothes!"

"Everything all right here?" A hockey fan, an adult sitting behind them. Jess nodded and pulled herself together.

"Fine. Thank you." She glared at Nick. Lowered her voice. "That is *not* okay."

"The Legacy," Nick said.

Jess looked at him, puzzled. He opened his mouth to say something more, but at that moment, the public address system announced the National Anthem. Thousands of people stood. The men pulled off their hats. A recording artist named Lily Oyer, whose first solo release had dropped two days earlier, belted out a rendition that drew thunderous applause. The teams were introduced. It was too loud to think.

Nick followed the game, leaning forward, elbows on his knees. Jess had disappeared for him. The other seventeen thousand people in the arena were similarly transfixed—it was a sellout crowd now.

Jess leaned to her left. "What about the—"

But Nick held up a hand, silencing her. "Did you see that forecheck?"

"I know rain check, blank check, paycheck. Any relation?"

"Do you know *anything* about hockey?"

"It's played on ice. Each team has . . . six . . . players. They jump over walls a lot. Not sure what that's about. There's a puck down there somewhere, though I can't actually see it most of the time. The goalies look like they're wearing fat suits. The fans sound like they're really, really angry."

Nick took his eyes off the ice for the first time since the game had started. "That's good. Very good, actually."

She had him now. "What Legacy?" Jess asked.

A whistle blew. Music played.

"That's a TV timeout," Nick said.

"They take time out to watch TV?" Jess said.

"For the *ads*!"

"Oh, really?" As sarcastic as she could make it.

Realizing she'd gotten him, Nick softened, eyeing her with more respect. "Don't worry. I'm not going to report on this. Far as I'm concerned, we never met. It's better for both of us."

"Why? I mean, I'm happy to hear it, don't get me wrong. But why for you?"

"The Legacy," he said again, as if that meant something to them both.

With the game under way and the crowd completely absorbed, Nick drew closer to Jess. Amanda elbowed Tim, forcing him to switch seats. As Amanda leaned in, Jess reacted poorly to the physical contact, jerking away like a kid brushing off a troublesome little brother. Then she was upset with herself.

Keeping their three faces close together, Nick launched into an almost scholarly explanation of the early days of the company, how Walt and his brother Roy surrounded themselves with brilliant, creative minds, people who could help translate Walt's particular genius into practical, material goods, like animated films and theme parks. How Walt's love of magic, folklore, and fairy tales took the group on a ride from the ordinary to the sublime.

But not every employee proved him- or herself a perfect fit. Some creative types arrived with big egos, with a need for authorship and recognition. Some quickly, some over time, each revealed him- or herself to be incompatible with the kind of teamwork Walt demanded. People moved on; others were hired. Sometimes it was amicable, but sometimes not.

"A man named Amery Hollingsworth was fired by Roy in late 1948."

"Decommissioned," Jess said.

"What's that?"

"Never mind."

"In a newspaper interview at the time, Amery claimed he'd created the Evil Queen, Lady Tremaine, and Maleficent well ahead of their films coming out. It's pure bunk. Those characters were borrowed from Brothers Grimm and other stories, but don't tell Amery Hollingsworth that! His ego and his general attitude got him fired. He wasn't happy. He started bad-mouthing Walt and Roy and the company, spreading ugly rumors."

"Like someone else I know," Jess said.

Having no idea who Nick was or what he did, Amanda gaped, taken aback by Jess's rudeness.

"I avoid the ugly," Nick said in his own defense. "The rumors I spread are nice rumors. More like leaks— what's to come, what we can get excited about. I hate the negative stuff. Unlike Amery Hollingsworth. He was a parasite. He clung to his past with the company, was paid for slanderous magazine articles slamming

Walt and the company. He spread nothing but lies. The more successful the company became, the darker the lies. He sued Walt and Roy, sued the company, was constantly dragging them into court. It bankrupted him. He lost every suit, but still he kept hiring lawyers. He wouldn't stop. He became possessed, much like the characters he claimed to have created."

A shot on goal brought half the crowd to its feet. Nick paused, allowing the roar to subside. The cheers came and came, like waves crashing on the shore.

"His anger and resentment began the Legacy of Secrets. Hollingsworth was obsessed with bringing Walt and Roy down, obsessed with the dark characters he claimed he'd created. So he began what one Imagineer called the Campaign of Darkness. Even back then, there was evidence that the characters, good and bad alike, were more than just imaginary. Stories of sightings at the studios. Of direct encounters with ghosts and demons. The good characters showed up, too! Mickey sightings. Pluto. There are records. Not in Burbank, but somewhere."

Amanda poked Jess in the side. Jess knocked her hand away with a glare.

"These things had come alive. Whatever genius Walt had, it was stronger and more potent than he or his brother realized. He could make magic. It wasn't just a line, an ad. He really could make dreams come true. Call it a gift, a curse. It's all in how you look at it. And he used it for good. That's what's important. That's what it was all about for the Legends. The Happiest Place on Earth. Smiles. Family. Good times.

"Hollingsworth was the polar opposite. Where Walt loved magic, Hollingsworth studied alchemy. Undone by his hunger for fame and recognition, he made it his mission to find out if the ghosts and visions were real, and if they were, to learn how to control them."

"The Overtakers!" Amanda gasped. Nick nodded, his eyes wide and serious.

"The Legacy was the start of all that, yes. It's called the Legacy because Amery had a son. That son had three more sons. The Sleeping Beauty story goes back to the fourteen and fifteen hundreds. Evil forces have been a part of us, of human storytelling, for a long, long time."

"Who *are* you?" Amanda croaked out.

"Me? I'm just a guy. A kid, like you. I read a lot. I like to read. To study. To figure things out. So sue me."

"No, no!" Amanda said quickly. "Not at all! This is amazing."

Nick gave her a tentative smile.

"I don't own a phone, smart or not. I spend too much time in libraries and none at school dances. You can take all the sports in the world, just leave me hockey and soccer. I watched a hundred hours of the World Cup, most of it live. Tim Howard is my all-time hero, but I'm too small to play keeper."

"Keeper," Jess muttered. In spite of herself, she shot a look at Amanda.

The Ducks scored a goal, and what felt like an 8.2 earthquake shook the arena. Amanda jumped. Jess turned.

Nick said, "Oh, no!"

On the huge TV screen over center ice, where there should have been a shot of the crowd celebrating the goal, was a picture of the three of them: Nick, Jess, and Amanda. It hung on the screen too long, finally giving way to a replay of the goal.

"That's them," Nick said.

"Them?"

"The Legacy! You have to understand. Amery committed suicide, but not before infecting his son with his poison. It's only grown since then. We have to get out of here. Now. Right now. I guarantee you: they're already on their way."

"But, but . . ." Jess sputtered. "We're not doing anything wrong. Are we?"

No time to answer. Amanda spotted them first. "There!"

Three different security men were converging on their section from different spots, all a good distance away. Before any kind of plan could be made, Nick jumped up and left the girls, speeding down their row, angering the fans who were still celebrating the goal, his effort made all the easier because so many were already standing.

ANAHEIM, CALIFORNIA

The Tower Dorm

43

DOWN THE FAR REACHES of an unoccupied wing scorched decades earlier by blue-sky lightning, tucked into a recess that had once been a doorway but was now a charred arch, Jess looked up at Tim.

"Why did you do that? Why did you put me next to Nick?"

"Did you know there are sixteen million thunderstorms on Earth every year? That nearly two thousand storms are raging every minute of every day? Lightning can travel as far as twenty-five miles from its origin. That's how blue-sky lightning happens, and that's what hit this hotel and killed that family in the elevator—just like all the stories say."

"What were you really after in the basement?" Jess said, fixing him with a steady gaze.

He acted as if he hadn't heard her. "Nick says there's a rumor that these abandoned areas in the Tower are not as abandoned as they look. Says they're kept this way to keep us out, that the Imagineers use them for weird stuff."

"I'm going to use them to hide a body if you

don't start answering my questions," Jess said.

"I wanted you to hear it from him. That's all. I wanted you two to meet."

"You were after Legacy files." She still hadn't looked away, and now Tim met her eyes. His gaze was feverish, his cheeks bright with color.

"No, that's not true. Well, it's partially true, but it's way more than that. Look, CBS and NBC battled over color television transmission standards way back when. Nick has decent sources that claim some of the technology actually came out of Disney. Highly sophisticated stuff. That Disney could have made zillions if they'd held on to it and developed it themselves. So why didn't they?"

"I give up."

"Me too. Still, I wanted answers."

"You wanted answers about the Legacy, too."

"So what? I'm not allowed to be curious about more than one thing at once?"

"You're not allowed to lie."

"I didn't lie."

"Not telling the truth is the same thing as lying."

Tim threw up his hands in exasperation. "Do you always tell the truth, Jess? Do any of us *always* tell the truth? We can't! Truth is like a bar of soap: you try too hard to hold on to it, and it squirts away. We all have secrets. Truth and secrets are two different things. Don't confuse them."

"Secrets are truths. Don't try to pretend otherwise." Jess paused, unsure of her next question, of what it might reveal. "How much do you believe about the Legacy?"

"All. I believe it all. It just makes sense to me. And I think there may be files on this guy Hollingsworth down there. You put something like that in the Burbank archives and it gets found. You bury it here, in a room filled with old exams; who's going to even look?" He lowered his voice—spoke so quietly that he gave Jess chills. "They upgraded that basement area, don't forget. Coincidentally, it was just in the past couple of years, when your friends the Keepers were fighting off the villains. I think they had to hide the really important stuff. Everything about Disney is so public. And yes, a lot of that is because of people like Nick. I get that. But every warehouse, every piece of property, every *lamp* has been documented. So where do you hide the secrets?"

"Out in the open. Wayne always said to hide things in the open."

"Or in the basement of a dormitory you happen to own, where no one ever goes. You upgrade some robots, put an old guy in charge of running them, and let the bloggers go wild."

"I was asking about the Legacy," Jess reminded him, though her voice was slightly softer now, and she had uncrossed her arms.

"It's all connected. The answers about the Legacy, if they exist, are in that storage room. If they were—"

"Shh!"

Voices. Two women coming toward them from deeper down the burned-out hallway.

"I'm saying this," said one, in a low, rich voice. "What is fair to the student? I understand the company's position, but in the case of—"

Jess didn't hear the rest because her ears started ringing the moment Tim kissed her. It was on-the-lips, his hand gently behind her neck. Her legs went weak, and she sank. He caught her, and she found herself kissing him back without really meaning to. The two women walked past, so engaged in conversation, they didn't see them kissing.

She assumed Tim was kissing her to give them an excuse to be "out of bounds" if caught. Yet, his kiss didn't feel like an excuse, and hers certainly wasn't.

The kiss stopped. He whispered warmly into her ear, "Sorry about that."

Not me, Jess wanted to say, feeling her face burn. "That was quick thinking," she said instead, trying to catch her breath.

"You . . . I mean, we . . ." Tim stammered. He looked like he'd been slapped awake from a deep sleep. He leaned back, uncomfortable. ". . . that . . . It was just—"

"I know," Jess said.

He leaned in toward her ever so slightly.

"Hey!" she said, pushing him away. "Get hold of yourself."

"Yeah . . . right! Of course."

"You owe me an apology, but there's no need to apologize. And that's all I'm going to say about it. Okay?"

Tim looked confused, but nodded slowly.

"Did you hear what they were talking about?"

He shook his head. "I didn't hear *anything*," he said.

Jess bit back a grin. She wasn't going to let him see it, see how happy he'd just made her. "The word 'legacy' means a gift or birthright. It's something passed on."

"Yeah."

"I want to know what you and Nick know."

"You mean, are there other Hollingsworths? Is that what you're asking? Because I don't know, Jess. Was the guy as nasty as Nick says? I don't know that, either."

"But if I could get the files?" she proposed. Her own words shocked her even as she uttered them.

"Never gonna happen," Tim said. "I heard Langford held both Emily and Amanda after classes."

"What? Is that why Mandy wasn't on the four o'clock shuttle? I thought she was in conference."

"I think she *is* in conference . . . with Langford, and probably Bernie Crenshaw." Tim stepped away, leaned out into the hallway to look in either direction. "They're gone. What do you mean about *you* getting the files?"

"I never said that. Forget I said that."

"You didn't want anything to do with that."

"And I still don't! Look, Tim, is Nick for real? Is the Legacy for real?"

"Nick, yes. The Legacy? How should I know? And hey, calm down. It's not like it's a matter of life or death."

Jess said nothing.

"Right? Jess . . . *right?*"

She looked at Tim with sad, crestfallen eyes and answered in a sullen voice. "I'm not so sure."

44

THE FREEZE-FRAME VIDEO SHOWED giant cards flying wildly in all directions, scattering among a throng of Disneyland guests. Although shot from a security camera at a distance, the people were recognizable.

Amanda saw herself in the crowd, hands outstretched. She remembered that moment clearly.

Tobias Langford had made her take a seat in the conference room, empty but for the two of them and another woman who sat in the corner behind Amanda. This woman had not been introduced, nor had she spoken. Langford stood a few feet from Amanda, looking tall and angry.

"That is you. There's no denying it. The cards are flying, which is you as well, I'm assuming. You've used your—power? your ability?—in public *inside one of our parks*. You have done so without permission and apparently with little regard for our guests."

Amanda clutched the edge of the office chair to keep her arms from shaking. "Excuse me, sir, but Peggy, the assistant dean, told me to use what you all brought me here for. That's all I was doing. Ask her, if you want."

Langford looked cornered and unsure how to answer. Instead, he played the video. A moment after the cards flew, the sword raised by the Jack of Hearts floated up into space and then clattered heavily to the ground. The crowd parted, seemingly of its own will, and people moved in a wiggling line as if they were being shoved out of the way by an invisible force.

"And that is Emily Fredrikson, is it not? In her invisibility project." Langford began pacing. "Well? Speak up, girl! Don't lie to me! If you want to remain at DSI, you had better start talking. *Right now!*"

"Who is she?" Amanda said, her voice shaky. She jerked her head back at the woman behind her as she spoke. Questions, too many questions, swam in Amanda's head. Why hadn't Langford said anything about the cards coming alive, for one? It felt like he didn't want to bring up the subject of Overtakers in front of this other woman, and that made Amanda wonder why not.

"An observer. Never mind her."

"What, is she here to make sure you don't hit me?"

"I don't hit. I don't bite. Tell me about the basement. Ah! Your eyes flared just now. You know exactly what I'm talking about. You and Emily in the basement. Why?"

Amanda considered how to lie without, well, not

telling the truth. "I don't like basements. They remind me of a place near Baltimore that I don't like one bit. Not a big fan."

"Emily has perfected her invisibility suit, hasn't she? That's why the sword in the video appears to float."

"You'd have to ask her."

"Do you deny having been in the dorm basement?"

"I told you: I don't like basements. Have I heard stories about Dirk? Yes. But everything's a story with Disney."

"Fine, then. Let's start there. How about I tell you a story?" Langford braced his hands on the table and leaned in toward Amanda. She jutted her chin, staring right back.

"Another time, maybe? I'm gonna be late for the four thirty shuttle." She appealed directly to the stone-faced woman behind her. If Amanda had guessed right, it was her job to make sure Langford didn't harass her in any way. "I need to get back to the dorm for personal reasons," she added.

"What were you after down there?" Langford said, refusing to yield. "Who sent you? Was it hazing? Or something more . . . directed? These are important questions we need answered, Miss Lockhart!"

"No one told me to do any such thing," Amanda said honestly. Philby had told her where she might find the files, sure, but not that she had to go get them. That had been her choice entirely.

"There's more going on here than you realize. That invisibility suit is the property of this company. Ms. Fredrikson is required to obtain written permission to operate any such device outside of this teaching facility. Did she tell you that? Did she tell you what kind of trouble you'd be in for assisting her?"

"The only slightly related thing I've heard is that the school administration values *transparency*," Amanda said, raising an eyebrow.

The woman behind her coughed with what sounded like amusement, but quickly recovered.

Langford's face had started to mirror the American flag on the wall: red skin, white eyeballs, blue eyes. He leaned in so close that Amanda could smell his coffee breath. "Let me advise you, young lady! Sixty-eight seconds before you're seen doing . . . whatever it is you do in this video, we observe an atmospheric anomaly over a particular carousel horse. It's what we call 'oil.' That phenomenon coincides, on the following rotation, with the identification of two Disney employees whose role in the company is known as DHI. I believe you know these individuals as the Kingdom Keepers. I believe you call them your friends."

He straightened, clasped his hands behind his back,

and fixed Amanda with a withering gaze. In spite of herself, she squirmed.

"You are associating with the wrong people, Miss Lockhart. This oil, this phenomenon, is of major interest to the company. It has cost us downtime on our attractions. It has baffled some of the most brilliant minds Disney employs. You have signed confidentiality agreements, so I don't mind sharing this with you. We *will* get to the bottom of it. When we do, anyone who has not come forward will be in grave danger of losing not only *her* standing here at DSI, but may face criminal and civil lawsuits as well. Do I make myself clear?"

"Is that another pun on *transparent*?"

The observer slipped again, barking out a laugh. Encouraged, Amanda added, "The four thirty? I really *need* to be on that shuttle."

"Go!" Langford barked the word so loudly that Amanda jumped.

Collecting herself, she rose out of her chair. Nearing him on her way to the door, she spoke as softly as she could. "I would never, *ever*, do anything to hurt this company. If you've read my application, I think you know that."

She slipped out the door before he responded, before he could call her back and ask her to explain.

45

"YOU LOOK AWFUL," Jess said, from her bed.

"So we're speaking now?" Amanda replied, dropping her backpack with a thud and collapsing onto her own bed.

"Don't, okay?"

"You've been treating me like dog dirt. What do you expect?"

"I have not."

"I am not interested in Tim, Jess. You've got that all wrong."

"I've had a lot of things wrong."

"So now you want to pretend they never happened?" Disbelief radiating from Amanda's every word. "It doesn't work like that."

"Look, Mandy, not everything revolves around you, as surprising as that may be."

"Seriously? This is us making up?"

"I didn't say we were making up, did I? Have you apologized? Have I? Though I will if you want." Jess paused, and then added in a gentler voice, "Honestly, this bites. I hate this."

"Yeah? Well, me too." Amanda rolled up onto an elbow, tried to make out Jess's features in the dark. "I got grilled by Langford. He has park video of me pushing the cards. He suspects Emily and I were in the basement, too. I assume I should start packing." Headlights flashed outside; in their brief glow, she got her first good look at Jess. "Whoa! Talk about looking awful. What's with you?"

"What was it Wayne told the Keepers? The most recent message?"

"You know perfectly well."

"Mandy, come on. What . . . was . . . it?"

"Gosh, Jess! You don't have to treat me like I'm a simpleton. It's funny; Charlene gets that treatment from so many people. Just because she's pretty, what, she can't think? So don't start doing it to me." Amanda paused, and her voice dropped, trembled a bit. "Besides, I'm not that pretty."

"You're gorgeous. Stunning. And you'd better know it, though I'm glad you never seem to. Why are we even talking about this? Do you think I'm jealous?"

"There . . . is . . . nothing . . . to—"

"I know! I got it!"

"Then what?"

"What was Wayne's most recent mes—"

" 'It's about time.' "

"Correct," Jess said.

"So what?"

"Some things bear repeating."

"I know that expression," Amanda said. "Mrs. Nash used to lay that on us all the time."

"Yes, she did. When did she use it?" Jess's voice was steady and calm. She was leading them somewhere, but for the life of her, Amanda couldn't see the destination.

"When she was trying to hammer something into us."

"Correct."

"What is this, a quiz? What's going on, Jess?"

"Play along."

"With what?"

"Some things bear repeating *to others*." Jess rolled off her bed, got up, and closed the window shades, casting the room into pitch darkness.

"Wait a second! You're not quizzing me. You're trying to tell me something."

Jess said nothing. She flipped on the desk lamp beside her; as she did, she allowed a casual smirk to cross her face—a look that confirmed Amanda's theory.

"You can't tell me something, but you need to tell me something." Amanda had sat up too, was leaning forward, every inch of her body quivering with intensity.

"There are limits on all of us."

"Limits," Amanda said, deciphering. Decoding. "'Repeating to others.' The Keepers." She waited. "Oh, come on. A wink? You smiled just now. Do it again." Another pause. "You're not going to, are you?"

Jess shook her head gently.

"That must have been some oath!"

Amanda was onto something. She could tell by the way Jess nodded.

"The paperwork when we enrolled? No one really takes that ser—"

Jess shook her head, cutting her off.

"Oh. I see."

Jess nodded.

"Limits. The Imagineers are upset about the carousel, the cards. I *know* that much. Langford's so ticked off by all of it he could start a fire with his eyes. The Keepers have pushed the limits too far."

Was she onto something? Jess just stared, her eyes fixed on the far wall of their room. Amanda racked her brain, desperate to come up with some—any—answer. "Oh, please!" she exploded. "Come on."

Jess remained unflinching, unmoving.

"Limits . . ." Amanda repeated the word several times. "'It's about time' bears repeating *to the Keepers*. They're being investigated . . . attacked . . . limited . . . switched off."

Jess's eyes flared unintentionally. She looked to the floor, where Amanda's dirty laundry lay in a heap. "You really should do your laundry at least once a month."

"Don't change the subject."

"What subject? I haven't said anything."

"This is a stupid game."

Jess shrugged.

"Switched off? Why? Is it because the OTs are back?"

"Don't know what you're talking about," Jess said. "We're *done* here, all right?"

"Done?" Amanda's face expressed surprise so strong it bordered on outrage. "We're done." Her voice quieted again as the meaning sank in. "No. *They're* done. Finn? Philby?"

"We've got *five* great friends."

"All of them! You want me to contact all of them. They're in trouble?"

"They're always in trouble," Jess said, shrugging and reaching for the desk lamp. But she didn't turn it off, not yet.

"Time is running out," Amanda whispered.

"Who can stop it?"

"Their time is limited. Someone's going to stop something. I need to tell everyone." Amanda looked as if she might jump out of her bed and run out the door.

From her position by the desk, Jess sighed, releasing a flood of pent-up tension. She hung her head like a marathoner at the end of a long race. "It's good to be talking again," she said, stepping forward across the laundry-strewn floor and grinning as Amanda accepted her hand.

ORLANDO,
FLORIDA

46

"WE CAN'T TELL ANYONE," Philby said. He spoke with biting authority. "Not our parents, not Wanda, not Joe. No one."

The five Keepers had come together in a video chat room. On the screen, each face was roughly the size of a playing card.

"The clothes are important," Finn said. "Thrift stores. Costume shops. There isn't a lot of time."

"What exactly is the rush?" Charlene sounded peeved. She'd missed a fancy party to attend the conference, and was still sulking about it.

"We don't know, but we've been warned," Philby said. "Amanda was very clear. She thinks maybe something's being shut down. One of the parks? The DHIs? Who knows? For maintenance? Security? It doesn't really matter. The point is to get across, find Walt's pen, and get it where it needs to be."

"What Philby means is . . . or, I should say, what it's important we all understand," Willa addressed the group as a whole, "is that if whatever's going on includes shutting down the projectors, it's probably going to be a day or two or more until we return."

"My show's on hiatus for ten days," Charlene said, reminding them for the fourth time. "It sucks, you guys. I wanted to get back home and be with you all. But I'll tell my mother I have to do some looping, that it's going to be another day or two. Any more than that, she's going to freak."

"Ten days! Look," Philby said, "the whole idea is that we do this quickly. That's why the five of us have to go together."

"Right," Charlene said. Her face had become more expressive as her acting career blossomed. Right now, it expressed her contempt for everything Finn claimed was true about time travel.

"It's worth a try, don't you think?" Maybeck said, pleading with Charlene. "Plus, hey, we get to hang out."

Finn suppressed a smile. Clearly, Maybeck didn't mean the Keepers as a whole. He meant he'd get time with his girlfriend.

"I'm just saying," Charlene said. "We can't put off trying to return. And if it doesn't work, we keep trying. We can't get stuck, you guys."

"Of course not!" Philby said, waving a hand as if to brush Charlene's objections away. "To be safe, we're bringing two Returns. I made one that works off transistors." He held the new device up to the video camera on his laptop. It was about the size of a box of butter, much clunkier than the key fob to which the Keepers were accustomed. "I won't bother you with the details. But it runs off the radio spectrum in use back then."

Charlene sighed, slumped her head into her hands. "God, this time travel nonsense . . . Willa and I have to wear skirts? Seriously?"

"Stop whining, Charlene. We have to wear chinos and button-down shirts, or work clothes."

"Philby's talking to me, Charlie," Maybeck said. "Look, I'm not thrilled, either. African-Americans were called 'coloreds' back where we're going. If I'm going to be in the park, it'll have to be as a worker."

"That's awful!" Willa said, crinkling her brow.

"That's America in the fifties," Finn said. "Land of the free. Home of the brave."

"I can handle it." On the screen, though, Maybeck winced visibly. "Just remember, you guys can't be too friendly with me. Polite, but not chummy. Especially you, Charlie."

They all complained as one, but after a minute Philby called them to order. "Maybeck brings up a good point. If it really is back then and not now—and I believe you, Finn—but if it is, we have to be super careful about expressions: how we talk, how we act. Everything was different in the nineteen fifties. Half the stuff we have today, from plastic to GPS to our phones, didn't exist or looked a lot different. Air conditioners weren't that common. The running shoe hadn't evolved. That's why we'll wear leather shoes or white Keds sneakers when we cross over. There's no spandex or Sharpies. The peanut M&M is only a couple years old, and it just comes in the tan color." Gasps all around.

"If we slip up on that stuff, we're going to stick out. And we're already going to stick out." His mouth twisted. "Being black-and-white, I mean."

"Wayne asked for two days," Finn said. "We've given him that. Maybe we won't be black–and-white. Maybe he managed to fix it."

"Some of us could have messed-up memory," Willa said. "Like what happened to Maybeck, and Finn, the first time they traveled. We've got to go with whatever Finn says." She aimed this directly at Philby, though she didn't use his name. "Dell will find a way to return us. One day, maybe two, and then we're back."

"Our parents are going to freak," Philby said.

"Especially when they see how we're dressed," Maybeck added.

"But at least they've been through it before," Finn said. "They'll know what's going on."

"Not my roommate," Charlene said. "I mean, she

knows about us, but I'm not going to tell her what we're doing."

"Tell her you're exhausted," Philby said. "I'll return you before the rest of us if we have to."

Charlene nodded, though she didn't look at all convinced.

"All good?" Finn said. No one complained. "Pleasant dreams, you guys. See you on the other side."

ANAHEIM, CALIFORNIA

Disneyland

47

Explosions cracked the air and shook the earth. Philby sat up quickly, struggling to collect himself.

A crowd. Children and families, laughing and clapping. Music. Fireworks.

"Disneyland," Philby mumbled.

"No place better!" A complete stranger said back to him. The exceptionally hairy man wore a sleeveless undershirt with a sweat-stained image of Bob Parr from *The Incredibles* on the front. He eyed Philby's outfit. "*Newsies*? Am I right?"

Philby remembered Finn's description of 1950s Wayne, how he'd made the same comparison. "Right as rain, sir!" An expression he'd learned from his grandparents. The man smiled and nodded.

Central Plaza teemed with thousands of onlookers. Orchestral music swelled; cymbals crashed. As planned, most people were looking up, not down at the ground where Philby had materialized. As always, it took him a minute to fully inhabit his DHI, to establish his surroundings and make the mission real in his mind. He looked around for the others, only realizing belatedly that they could be three yards from him and he still wouldn't see them.

No time to waste. Now came the tricky part: moving through the crowd as a DHI without passing *through* people.

He closed his eyes, concentrating. It didn't take a lot of thinking to get fear and anxiety to overtake him. All Philby had to do was consider the possibility that he was about to time travel. It bothered him that losing memory was critical to his well-being. He didn't want to forget one second of what was about to happen. But he accepted his fate.

Lost in thought, Philby bumped shoulders with a small woman. He apologized, but hid a smile: a good sign; he'd lost some of his hologram already.

He was on the front end of Central Plaza, past the Partners statue, when he first spotted the Dapper Dan stalking him. The Cast Member was a good twenty yards away, standing on the sidewalk, but Philby felt the almost palpable existence of a string connecting the two of them. Moving precisely, the Dapper Dan matched his progress nearly stride for stride.

To Philby's left, Jack Skellington and Sally walked away from the castle, tracking him and the Dapper Dan. It wasn't as if they were the only ones heading down Main Street toward Town Square, but once again they seemed invisibly connected to Philby, pacing along with his every step.

"Dell!" Willa's voice, coming from behind him. He didn't want to bring her into this. Jack Skellington gave Philby the creeps, and Sally was no looker, either. If they were Overtakers, not Cast Members, he was in trouble. For one thing: if Jack was already dead, could he be hurt or killed? How could you fight the already dead?

Philby raised a closed fist—the Keepers' hand signal for *stop*. Hopefully Willa would get the message.

He took it as his responsibility to distract his stalkers. No matter what, the rest of the Keepers had to make it to Walt's apartment as quickly as possible. The park was closing. They had only a brief window in which to start the music box and reach the carousel before their presence would invite security.

Distract. Was a good defense the best offense, or the other way around? He couldn't remember! Philby turned abruptly and ran through the crowd, heading straight for Jack Skellington. As he did, he pushed all fear away.

* * *

Willa saw Philby's raised fist and stopped. A few heartbeats later, she spotted the Dapper Dan, a man who seemed curiously out of place and awkwardly alone, despite being situated in the heart of Disneyland. She moved onto the same sidewalk, staying behind him, making sure he stayed in sight and ahead of her.

She didn't know whether to trust him or not. As Cast Members in decidedly human form, the Dappers walked a line between fantasy and reality. Worse, they were adults.

It didn't take long to be sure that the Dapper was stalking Philby. He was pathetically bad at it, turning his whole head in Dell's direction, instead of just his eyes; slowing when Philby slowed, moving as Philby moved. She quickly became suspicious.

The thick crowd bobbed and surged on all sides, preventing her from spotting Jack Skellington and Sally. Philby was headed toward the two in full stride, brimming with the determination she'd come to love about him. When he put his mind to something, nothing could stand in his way. Though concern pained through her chest and briefly stole her breath, she found herself feeling sorry for Jack and Sally.

She had work to do. Two against one was bad odds for Philby. She couldn't be sure of the Dapper's intentions, but if hostile it only made things worse. She aimed to stop him, stepping off the sidewalk, charging through the mass of people, powered by a feverish impulse to help her boyfriend.

* * *

"What?" Philby demanded, stepping up and confronting Jack Skellington head-on.

The gourd-headed figure threw his gangly arms in the air, expressing surprise. Philby's confidence had his DHI tingling, a sensation he took to be a positive sign. He stepped through Jack, spun around, and spoke again.

"I'm back here, clown face."

Skellington spun.

"What do you want with me?" Philby said.

The black and white creature lowered his head—he was a good deal taller than Philby's DHI—putting his face only inches from Philby's. He waggled a long, boney finger. The gesture spoke clearly to Philby: *Oh, no you don't. I'd be careful if I were you! You're asking for trouble if you go through with it.*

Philby attempted to step through the figure again, but this time he chest-bumped Skellington, knocking him back.

"That wasn't very nice," Sally said.

"You stay out of this!" Philby admonished her.

"I most certainly will not, mister! Jack and I are one and the same. Birds of a feather. Where he goes, I go. Jack's a good man! Dead or not! You keep that in mind."

Philby addressed the bobblehead, his voice flat and

calm. "Tell whoever sent you here that we will not turn back. Not now. Not ever. That's all you need to say. All they need to hear."

"I'm sure Jack has no idea what you mean," said Sally.

"I'm pretty sure he does." Philby had not flinched, not once since going head-to-head with the cadaverous puppet. "He meant to hurt me, or distract me, and he's been successful, at least in the second part. As for hurt—well, that'll be on him and all those he represents."

Spinning, Philby pointed across the street to the Dapper Dan, who was fast approaching. "Including you!"

The Dapper Dan stopped. He looked confused. Put off. Surprised.

Willa walked around the Dapper and addressed him. "If you, or any of your kind, follows us or keeps us from entertaining the guests, you will come to regret it."

"My kind?" he asked, incredulous.

She read his name tag: EZEKIEL.

Though her voice was calm and strong, her mind was spinning. She couldn't bring herself to imagine that the powerful Overtakers were behind this. The presence of Jack, Sally, the Dapper—it all felt, like the card attack on Finn had felt, like stragglers, isolated villains attempting to run interference without any leadership or plan.

"Jack!" she added, letting her tone show her exasperation, "You're supposed to be a good guy. Don't give in to a bunch of losers!"

Skellington stood up straighter. At his side, Sally took a deep, rasping breath. "How can someone who's already dead," she said, "lose anything?"

"You and any of the other leftovers, stay away from us!" Philby said, squaring his shoulders.

"And if you don't," Willa warned, "you'd better bring it." She spoke loudly, to make sure the Dapper Dan heard her as well. What kind of dumb name was Ezekiel?

The Dapper, unfazed, stepped forward. His face was solemn and composed. "Young lady, how horribly mistaken you are. I have, in fact, come to help."

"I'm sure!" Willa nearly spit at him.

She and Philby turned and walked away, moving hand in hand up Main Street USA toward Town Square. Philby's hand trembled. Willa's was ice cold.

Slowly, with a habit learned through years of adventure, they began to go all clear.

"What got into you?" Philby gasped.

"'It's about time,'" Willa replied, her DHI grasping his hand tightly. Not letting go.

48

FROM WALT'S APARTMENT, where Philby marveled at the music box, to the five Keepers running for King Arthur Carrousel, carried away by a sense of group adventure that had been sorely lacking in the past months, all dressed in period clothing, playing DHI tricks like jumping *through* the Partners statue while laughing at the top of their lungs, from this exhilarating dash, the Keepers arrived at the carousel and swarmed the platform of spinning horses.

There was merriment in the air, that rare and welcome rush that comes from perfect friendship. As the five awkwardly mounted Jingles, having drawn a small group of fans and onlookers, they held to each other's waists like a group of kids riding a toboggan. Maybeck, the last, was barely able to keep from sliding off the painted horse's rump.

Closing their eyes, some under the spell of heightened anticipation, others fighting off the fear that came with something new, the fear that could compromise their DHI and corrupt their chance to be part of this, whatever this was.

They vanished.

The few park guests who had identified one or another of the Kingdom Keepers and had followed so eagerly to the carousel clapped and cheered, celebrating what they thought was a magic show. Jingles looked lonely, rotating round and round as the park cleared for the night. The security camera's time lapse captures would show an emptying Fantasyland, families departing for the long ride home, Cast Members closing and cleaning, an enchanted space being readied for the following morning.

There would be no more sightings of the five kids who'd climbed aboard Jingles, holding on for dear life, their eyes shut as if anticipating something wonderful.

BURBANK,
CALIFORNIA

⋊⋉Is the past really in the past
Or is it still to come
Is the future what's in store for us
Or has it already begun
Is the present really happening
Or will it never come*

---

*Wind_Princess

49

"THANK YOU FOR MAKING IT on such short notice," Joe Garlington said from the other side of three display screens connected to his computer. He rolled his chair out from behind them, though he remained on the far side of the desk.

"No problem," Amanda said dryly. She sipped from the water the secretary had given her. Coughed.

"We both know better than that," Joe said. "I heard from Toby Langford."

"Oh."

"And of course, I'd seen the video as well. You and the cards. The push."

"Mr. Langford didn't mention them," Amanda said, sitting forward in spite of herself. "Did you know that? Why wouldn't he acknowledge that there was an attack?"

Joe scribbled a note. "Don't change the subject, Amanda."

"What is the subject?"

"I think you know."

"Finn's not answering my texts."

"That's not the subject. Protecting secrets and

keeping secrets are two different things. We require you to protect our company secrets. We ask you not to lie or do things, things *like public displays of supernatural ability*, that will bring the company bad publicity."

Amanda sat back, stung. "Don't you want your guests believing in the magic?" she said softly. ᛉJoe knew about the battles between Overtakers and characters. He knew the Disney villains were real and that a band of holographic teenagers really did cross over at night.* Certainly, he must believe in the magic, she thought.

"Do you think this is a good time to be sarcastic with me?"

"Probably not."

"No probably about it." Joe jotted down some more notes. Amanda didn't like that. She wished she could see what he was writing. "Tell me about it."

"It?"

"Careful," he warned.

"I've texted him for two days and nothing. That's completely unlike him."

His face reddened. "We're not talking about your love life, Amanda. We're talking about the carousel. The cards. You just happened to be there?"

---

*Lost_Technology

"I tried the others, too. Maybeck. Willa. Philby. Nothing. So I thought, heck, I'll just call Charlene. Voicemail. Where are they, Joe? Where have they gone?"

"Where did those cards come from?"

"Mad Hatter, I assume. They were going to hurt my friends. The Queen of Hearts is seriously psycho. What would you have done? Peggy told me to—"

"Don't give me that excuse. You and I both know Peggy was referring to your work at DSI, not inside the parks. Not with guests in attendance. You tried that line on Toby, I hear." Joe closed his notebook, looked at her wearily. "Please, Amanda, give me some credit. We accepted you and Jess into DSI as adults. That means we expect adult behavior and adult communication. Do you think yourself capable of that?"

"Why would all five of them go off the grid?" Amanda remained persistent.

Joe sighed, and put the cap on his pen. "Okay. That's all. I guess I'll just have to give you the time to find out."

"What?"

"You're suspended from DSI."

"Excuse me?" Amanda felt like she was about to cry.

"You're out. Whether that's temporary or permanent is up to you."

"Permanent? I am so sorry, Joe! I didn't mean to—"

"That's exactly the point, Amanda: You did mean to. Of course you did. Everything you did was premeditated. That's the most annoying and telling part of this, quite frankly. That, and your blatant dishonesty."

"Ask me whatever you want. I'll tell you anything!"

"You'll take a break, young lady." Joe's face was like a piece of stone; his eyes were cold. "What you do with that time is up to you. If I were you I would think about what it is I want for my future."

"I don't want to leave DSI. I'm sorry about everything. They're my friends, you know? Real friends. The first friends Jess and I have ever really had."

"Jessica seems to be toeing the line quite well." Joe stood. Amanda didn't like that. It implied the meeting was over, that he really wasn't giving her a chance to argue. "You'll do with the next week as you see fit. I leave it up to you. Please figure out what's important to you, and then we can talk again."

Tears gushed down Amanda's cheeks, despite her best efforts to hold them back. "I didn't . . ." she sobbed. "I'm so sorry . . . Really . . . Really sorry."

"I don't like this anymore than you do," Joe said, putting his arm around her and guiding her gently to the door. "You and Jessica are special to me. Important. I have no doubt—none whatsoever—that you'll make the most of these next few days. You're a smart kid, Amanda. When we meet again, all will be forgiven, and we can both move on. Sound good?"

Amanda nodded, drawing in deep breaths between sobs.

"Things have a way of working out when we put our minds to it," Joe said.

"I was just trying to help," Amanda gurgled.

He patted her on the shoulder. "Well then, that's a good place for us to start next week when we talk. Keep that in mind. Let's start right there."

* * *

"He said I should serve as a kind of DSI ambassador," Amanda said to Jess later as she packed. "Convince some of the parents that this is a good place for their kids."

"Joe said that?"

Her stomach knotted. They didn't lie to each other, but here she was doing exactly that. "He said how great it would be to get as many of the Keepers here next semester as possible. That I was the perfect person to convince them."

"What if Finn doesn't want to see you?"

Amanda offered her sister a look. "Since when?"

"Yeah, I suppose. What did he say about them not answering texts?"

"He made me think maybe they've been doing something with the Imagineers that has their phones down." The lying became easier as she went. A troubling development. She didn't like herself right now. She knew Jess wouldn't like her, either. "I think by sending me back there, he's planning to let me see them in person. So no complaints."

"This has to do with the Legacy, doesn't it?" Jess asked. "You two talked about Hollingsworth and the Legacy."

"I swear, I said nothing." Finally, a speck of truth. She cherished it.

"You're not mad at me again, are you?" Jess sounded terrified.

"Why would I be?"

"Because they let me into the basement."

"I'm not supposed to know about that."

"Tim shouldn't have told you."

"Why didn't you?" Amanda asked, keeping her eyes fixed steadily on Jess's.

"Don't get mad."

"Why should I get mad?"

"We just worked everything out."

"We did. And now I get to go work everything out with Wanda."

"What does *that* mean?" Jess asked.

Amanda blushed. "Nothing. Look, I don't have some switch that can turn off my feelings! I'm scared for him."

Jess laid a gentle hand on her shoulder.

"I'm being completely real here, Mandy. This is honest. No tricks. No secret messages. I have no idea where they are, where Finn is, why he isn't texting you. I know as much, or as little, about the Legacy as you do. Tim passed a file to *you* to get to the Keepers. Not me. You must remember this stuff."

"Because you're trying to protect me?" Half statement, half question. This time Jess didn't take the bait.

"I'm trying to protect all of us, and that includes Finn and the Keepers." Jess paused, sighed. "It's not easy."

"I have to know," Amanda said.

"'Ask, and it shall be given you; seek, and ye shall find; knock, and it shall be opened unto you.' Matthew 7:7."

"Since when do you go around quoting the Bible?" Amanda stepped away from Jess, throwing up her hands in complete exasperation.

"I know maybe three quotes, and another three or four from Shakespeare. So sue me." Jess twisted her lips as if biting back a laugh. "I mean, they come in handy."

"You're mocking me with that verse."

"I'm trying to warn you to leave it alone, Mandy. Believe it or not, sometimes we just don't want to know. Think who Finn is. Charlie. Maybeck. They're more pioneers than holograms. If you think for even a minute that we know everything they've done, you're fooling yourself. If they wanted us to know what they were doing now, we would."

"And if they're in trouble?" Amanda caught Jess's eyes, saw again the flare of emotion her friend struggled to conceal. "You know something. A dream? You've dreamed something."

"Not about them. It's not them in trouble. It's about you. Us."

"Tell me."

Jess pursed her lips. "I can't. Not until I understand it. I've learned the hard way that if I share my dreams too soon it causes nothing but trouble."

"Are we in danger?"

"In the dream? Yes."

"But you won't tell me from who, or what, or why?"

Jess laughed, and Amanda with her. "We are so pathetic," Jess said. They shared feelings of camaraderie. Of sisterhood. Survival.

"Don't do anything stupid," Jess said.

"With me, I'm not sure that's possible."

They laughed again.

"I love you, you know?" Jess said. "More than anyone. More than any of this. Real love. The kind where I'd run in front of a bus to stop it from hitting you. That kind of love."

Amanda nodded, her eyes going shiny. "Shut up."

"I'm going to come get you if you mess this up." Jess gave her a fierce hug, holding her close. "Whatever you do, keep looking over your shoulder."

"Your dream."

"Maybe."

"You're really not going to tell me?"

"I'm not . . . I can't." Jess paused to think about it. "Though maybe, in a way, I already have."

50

THE FIVE KEEPERS AWOKE within moments of one another. It was snowing, but in an *Alice in Wonderland* sort of way: pink, blue, green, red, and yellow circular flakes swirling about, stirred by an unpredictable breeze.

Charlene thought she'd crossed over into the inside of a snow globe. Maybeck saw it as confetti, but try as he might to capture and hold on to a flake, he could not. Philby simply sat, staring, the professor at work. Like Maybeck, Willa tried to displace the colorful balls, batting them with her hands and blowing on them. Nothing.

Finn knew what the others did not. He alone paid no attention to the electric atmosphere, looking instead for the way out.

Beyond what he knew to be glass, a group of long workbenches could be seen through the colorful snow. Empty wooden stools as tall as skyscrapers rose alongside the worktables. A series of funnel lights like winged canopies hung from black wires as thick as phone poles. Looking in the opposite direction revealed a long, shrinking tunnel, from which the colorful balls seemed to emerge in steady streams.

"I've got it!" Finn cried, swatting at the colorful Ping-Pong–size balls as if they were annoying insects. "Come here, everyone."

The others joined him, and Finn explained breathlessly that they'd arrived in a picture tube—apparently color, this time—but in shrunken form. In one direction were the electronics; in the other, whatever space the television set occupied. He believed it was a workshop of some kind.

Judging by the soft light in the room and the fact that the funnel lights were not switched on, it was daytime. Try as the Keepers might to leave the picture tube, there were only two proven methods. The first was to stand tall, turn sideways, and jump. The second, to dive. In both cases, the slightest twitch of fear would confine one inside, as Finn had previously experienced. To attempt a face-first jump would result in a painful collision.

"Why do I have no idea what you're talking about?" Philby said. He looked uncharacteristically pale and nervous.

"The folder!" Finn said energetically, trying to shake his friend out of his stupor. "Wayne created a color television from that information we gave him! These stupid balls are pixels. The reason we all look so weird and low-resolution is that it isn't a very good picture. I wonder what that will mean once we leave here?"

"Down, boy," Maybeck said. "Let's get everyone out of here before we play twenty questions!"

Ignoring Maybeck's desire to leap first and ask questions later, Willa pressed Finn to explain his color television comment, which Finn did, patiently and in more detail. He should have remembered the memory loss and planned for it better. It was slowing them down.

"So," Willa said carefully to Philby, "for the time being, let's assume Finn is not playing a practical joke." She then presented Philby with a physics problem: would their highly charged particles require excessive energy to break free of the cathode ray tube, and if so, were they better off attempting the disconnect as solos or as a group?

"You're saying the loss of energy may cause a kind of brown-out within the circuitry," Philby said, his eyebrows drawing together in thought.

"Tube circuitry," Willa said. "Not yet transistor. If you brown-out a tube, with no capacitors to sustain it—"

"That's like a Fender guitar amp," Maybeck said, eyes widening. "When those things don't have enough power, they distort big time. It gets ugly fast."

"Meaning," Willa said to Philby, "any remaining high concentrations of energy—"

"Will degrade precipitously!" Philby clapped his hands together.

"You're getting away from me," said Charlene, wrinkling her nose. "Keep it in the ballpark, would you?"

Smiling at her friend, Willa explained that if, say, two of them jumped first, the remaining three might be caught in the equivalent of an electronic storm. The sudden drop in energy would push the system to hurriedly fire photons at the screen and thus fill the picture tube with what had gone missing. The DHIs left inside would find themselves facing a firing squad of high energy.

Philby added that the sudden drop in energy could cause the circuitry to "brown out" and overheat. The remaining DHIs would be degraded and diminished, and, if the system failed altogether, trapped.

"Lost," Willa concluded. "In a kind of electronic Sleeping Beauty Syndrome. Like when a computer crashes and the document you were working on is gone. You never get it back."

"Lost," Charlene whispered, looking wide-eyed at Maybeck.

"It's not that easy, though," Philby said, and presented a third possibility: the departure of all five at once might "fry" the television. "It could close the door we came through."

"We can turn around now," Finn said. "Before this goes too far. The return from here is to dive back into the picture tube." He gestured behind them. "When we were on Jingles, we felt ourselves being swallowed by a tunnel-like thing behind us, right? I think if we ran in that direction now, the same thing would happen. We'd return."

"That's my vote," said Charlene decisively. "Return while we still can. How did we even get here? I am so totally confused. Philby, maybe you can do calculations or something? Once we're back, I mean. I don't like where this is going."

"Vote," said Maybeck. "Hands up for diving into that workshop."

Four hands went up.

Finn grinned. "We did it, you guys!"

"Did what?" Maybeck asked skeptically.

"Followed Wayne's message. Made it here. You guys don't know what's going on right now—"

"I have *no idea* what's going on right now!" Philby sounded desperate.

"But Finn and I do," Maybeck said, "and it's ridiculously, amazingly incredible. We've done the impossible."

Most of all, Finn wanted to say, *you guys are stuck with me.*

But he kept the sentiment to himself.

"Okay." Charlene couldn't keep her voice from trembling. "Are we seriously not going back?"

"No way," Maybeck said. "You have any idea what's out there?" He pointed toward the workshop.

Philby looked and sounded bewildered. "I feel as if I should know, but for some reason I don't. I've got nothing."

"Then it's working," Finn said.

"I'm not going to fight you," Charlene declared. "And I'm sure as heck not going to be trapped in here alone."

"Wayne would want us to jump," Finn said. "Believe it or not, I'm not even guessing at that."

"I wish I knew what was going on!" Philby shouted.

"You will in a minute," Finn said. "Once we jump, we've made it to where Wayne wanted us. After that, who knows? But it has to be important. Super important."

"Ready? We go on three?" Maybeck said.

"Hands in front like diving into a pool," Finn said. "And make yourself as flat, as much of a plane, as possible."

"I've never been plain," Maybeck quipped. "P . . . L . . ."

"We got it!" Willa chided.

On the count of three, the Keepers ran and dove.

51

THE KEEPERS SKIDDED ACROSS the smooth cement floor like five swimmers who'd left the blocks only to discover that there was no water in the pool. Philby called out that they were two-dimensional. Charlene qualified his comment by pointing out that at least they were in color, not black-and-white. Maybeck told everyone to check out the items on the workbenches: bulky hand tools for the most part; the few electric pieces looked clunky, oversize, and retro.

"That's a hand drill," he said. "No wireless anything. This stuff is ancient."

"This *stuff* is the best money can buy." The voice came from alongside the main door, which swung closed with a bang. A kid, not much older than any of the Keepers, stood before them. He wore a tam, though only Maybeck, who remembered Finn's description of the kid, found this significant.

"Who are you?" Philby asked defensively.

"I'm betting it's Wayne," Maybeck said.

The others gasped.

"I remember Finn's *Newsies* thing," Maybeck

added, astonished. "I remember meeting you."

"Good," the younger Wayne said. "Then everything's working just peachy!" He turned to Finn. "Did you bring it?"

"We did," Finn said. "Yes." He produced the folder he'd crossed over with, one of the two Jess had retrieved from the dorm's basement. Wayne accepted it, and then slowly waved his hand through Philby. "Do you see that, Finn?" he said. "No more fuzzy-wuzzies. The image is stable. This is extra important to the next step."

"Wayne," Philby said. "Your last name wouldn't happen to be—"

"Kresky? Yes."

"So you're related to the Wayne we know?"

"I think I am," Wayne said, winking at Finn, "the Wayne you know."

"What day is it?" a bewildered Willa asked. "I mean, what's the date, the exact date?"

"July seventeenth, nineteen fifty-five."

"Black Sunday," Willa mumbled. "The International Press Preview."

"Impressive," Wayne said. "But why Black Sunday? It's delightful out there!"

Willa withheld any comment for the moment. Instead, she addressed Finn. "Am I supposed to believe this is actually nineteen fifty-five?"

Charlene chimed in, too. "Yeah, nice try. I mean it's a funny joke, a good prank, but can we all just get real for a second?"

"The same thing happened to me, guys," Finn explained. "I crossed over to the Carousel of Progress; ended up in the nineteen sixties, and I was . . . part of . . . one of the shows. I . . . I just refused to believe it. It's still hard to believe."

"Come on," Philby said. "If this is nineteen fifty-five, which is preposterous, by the way, and this is Wayne Kresky, then we just time traveled!"

"Correct," said Wayne.

"As if! Ha-ha!" Philby said. But he sounded nervous.

"Guys," Maybeck said. "This is not a joke."

"We met this kid last time," Finn said. "There were tons of TV people around."

"Darn tootin'! They're still out there," Wayne said, pointing toward the door.

"Let's say we play along for a minute." Charlene turned to face Finn, called all the Keepers into a huddle, and whispered, "Why would our Wayne have wanted us here?"

"Obviously, there's work to be done," Finn said. "He must need us, though it's possible this Wayne doesn't exactly know that yet."

"We did as he asked," Philby said. "Supposedly, I mean; I'm not saying I believe this. But if . . . this . . . is real, then we time traveled, just like Wayne wanted. We did what he asked. We succeeded. Isn't that enough?"

"It is for me," Charlene said.

"You all know Wayne," Finn said. "There's always more."

"I'm right here, pal,"

"What if we don't want any more?" Charlene asked, ignoring Wayne.

Willa frowned at her, and Charlene looked down at her feet. Willa then asked Finn if they were allowed to mess with the past—she was beginning to believe, Finn thought.

"I don't think there's a handbook," he said. "I mean we've all seen the movies where they're not supposed to change the future by changing the past. But how's that even possible?"

"You guys know I'm something of a Disney historian," Willa said. "I prefer that to 'geek,' if you don't mind." No one corrected her. "Is it okay if I ask this guy some questions?"

"Be my guest," Finn said.

They broke the huddle, and Willa stepped closer to Wayne. With small, controlled movements, she reached out for him. Her two-dimensional DHI hand passed through his. She concentrated, tried again, and managed to touch his sleeve.

"How would you like to appear incredibly smart?" she asked. "Clairvoyant, even?"

"I already feel pretty smart," Wayne said, smiling at her. "You're here, aren't you? But, I'm listening."

"When we step outside, it's going to be pushing a hundred degrees."

"Okee-doke! That right there is impressive."

"Asphalt was laid yesterday in the park."

"Go on." Wayne looked surprised, and maybe a little stressed, by her knowledge.

"In this heat, that asphalt is going to get soft enough that women's high heels will sink into it. You might want to put out signs warning the guests."

"This is *fun*!" Wayne said, rocking back on his heels, his sarcasm obvious from his tone. "Are you having fun, miss? 'Cause I sure am!"

"It's more dangerous than fun, Wayne. There's also going to be a gas leak in Fantasyland—it'll cause three of the Lands to close."

"Today? You know this?"

"This afternoon, in fact. And I do know. It's part of Disney history."

"Good golly. I hadn't thought about how this would work, exactly."

Philby stepped forward. "Enough, Willa. Wayne, whose idea was it to bring us here?"

"I don't know," Wayne said. "I got a letter. Addressed to me, on yellowed paper. Just showed up one day in my pigeonhole. Lost and found, it said. A simple note I wasn't supposed to share with anyone—anyone but you. It said some kids would just appear. He, whoever wrote it, he told me things—secrets—that made me look real smart. So I did what it said, and the boy . . . these two boys showed up two days ago. The letter said that would happen. It told me to keep watch."

Finn felt chills invade his DHI. "Wayne knew we'd do it. Figure out his message, figure out time travel. He trusted us." Turning, he addressed the others. "Do you realize how important it is, that we've accomplished this?"

"What else does the letter say?" Philby hadn't turned away from Wayne. His tone was urgent.

"I'm supposed to let you read it. I could go get it, I reckon."

"There's no time. *What else?*"

"It mentions the ink. The letter's written in ink! Did I tell you that? It says the visitors—you all—have to 'put the ink back into the well.' Now, what on God's green earth is that supposed to mean? A real puzzler, am I right?"

"So *that* is what's next," Finn said, with emphasis. He took the time to look at each Keeper individually, forcing him or her to meet his eyes. "The pen! That's why he wanted us here, *needed* us here."

"Placing Walt's pen," Maybeck said.

"We'll have to find it first!" Philby said. Finn could practically see the sparks flying around Philby's brain. "Probably have to steal it first!"

"Oh, we'll find it all right." At last there was determination in Charlene's voice. "And when we do, every villain in this park will be after us. We'll have to be ready."

Wayne's head was inside the television cabinet now; when he spoke, his voice was muffled and tinny, and no one understood a word. Finally, he came up for air, and Willa addressed him.

"The plumbers' strike?" She turned her back on Philby and ignored Finn's impatient gesture to be quiet.

"What about it?" Wayne said.

"It's going to leave Walt Disney with a choice between running water in the drinking fountains or the toilets."

"Already happened. He chose the toilets." Wayne sounded breathless. "I'm not sure I want the full answer to what I'm about to ask next, but . . . The note said you'd be from another time. Is that right?"

"That's right," Finn said. But his mind was conflicted; he was distracted by what Maybeck had said.

Walt's fountain pen. From the first time he'd stared at Walt's music box, Finn had known. Getting here was one thing. Now, there was something else. Something completely different.

"Gee whiz," Wayne slumped against the console, shaking his head.

"You kept the letter?" Philby asked.

"Of course. It said to. That it had to be kept nice and private. Secret-like, except for when I showed it to you."

"Do you have it?"

"Like I said, not on me."

"Is it possible for a DHI to faint?" Charlene asked.

"It is!" Finn said. "I found out the hard way." He and Maybeck helped Charlene sit down. As they did, they exchanged a look. *Get ready*, it said. *Fasten your seat belt.*

"What are the odds," Maybeck said, "of us being the only ones who want that pen?"

Finn nodded deliberately. The gesture told Maybeck he agreed, but that their fears should be kept between them—at least for now. Though they exchanged no words, it felt as if they'd had an entire conversation.

On the other side of the group, Willa couldn't

stop with her history lesson. "They've issued fourteen thousand tickets to the international press for today's showcase. Well, those tickets have been counterfeited. *Twenty-eight thousand* guests are going to show up, swarm the park, and overwhelm everything you have planned."

"I think I need to sit down, too." Wayne found a sawhorse to lean against, wiped at the sweat that had beaded on his forehead.

"That's why today is known as Black Sunday," Willa explained.

"You could only know that if it had already happened," Wayne said.

"Right. And if you tell your bosses what I'm telling you now, you're going to look very smart."

"If I tell my bosses, they'll put me in an asylum."

The Keepers chuckled. All but Charlene, who had her head between her legs and was taking fast, shallow breaths. Maybeck stroked her back.

Beside them, Finn couldn't keep his thoughts from racing ahead. He and the Keepers would be easily identified if Wayne couldn't use the newly delivered information to create three-dimensional DHIs, a technology that wouldn't arrive into history for another decade at least. He felt the odds stacked badly against them. While the others joked, he shuddered.

"Look, we can't help but feel good about what we've accomplished," Philby said. "But I'm . . . apprehensive about going outside. Even if I won't remember it, I'm not sure it's smart or safe."

"We should start with the letter," Finn said, forcing himself to focus. "We need to read the letter."

"We're not going back. Are we?" Charlene had sat up. She looked terrified, pale and ghostly. "He tricked us, right? He always tricks us."

"Of course we're going to return!" Finn said. "Whenever we want."

He walked to the color television and held his fingers up to the screen. "See?"

But instead of his hand disappearing into the picture tube, his fingers poked the glass, skidded away. Finn tried a more perpendicular angle: the same result.

"No need to panic," Wayne said. "It's most likely something simple. The vacuum tubes don't last long, for instance." He moved to the large console in the back of the television and began tinkering.

"We're not going back," Charlene repeated. "I knew it. The minute I saw that we grew big like this, coming through there, I just knew it."

"It's the tubes," Wayne repeated. "I'll have it fixed in a jiffy!"

A puff of smoke rose from the television, and the screen went black. Charlene gave a low wail.

Wayne poked his face around the console. He wore a rueful expression.

"Or, if it's more complicated, then in due time."

"I don't think that's what we want to hear," Maybeck said, still hovering protectively near Charlene.

"I got a tip that we had to hurry if we were going to cross over manually," Finn told the group. "If we were back in our time, you'd remember that. But by now, I suppose you've forgotten. We voted, though."

"Sure we did," Charlene said, discouraged.

"We've got to believe him," Willa said. "Keep it together, everyone!" But her own voice sounded shrill.

"You're the one screaming," Charlene said.

"Am I? Oh, man!" Willa shrank into herself, leaned toward Philby.

"It's going to be all right." Wayne sounded a little too glee-club, a tone that didn't match the bewildered look in his eyes.

"Maybe it will, maybe it won't." Maybeck walked to the door and looked outside. "Part of me is excited to be here, now, to get to be a part of all this. Part of me is not okay with it at all."

"Wayne," Finn said. "I mean, with present company excluded—Wayne has always come through for us. We deciphered his message and we pulled off the impossible. It's nineteen fifty-five, people! And we're here!"

Maybeck spoke a word that turned present-day Wayne's face crimson.

Finn hardly heard. Something outside that door was pulling at him, just as he could feel it pull at the rest of the Keepers. Something extraordinary. The past. Something terrifying. Their present. A challenge. Young Wayne, old Wayne; their mentor and now their potential ally. Walt Disney himself.

"You understand what's out there?" he said. "Who's out there?"

No one answered.

"It isn't about going back. It never is," Willa said.

Finn knew what was behind him, but he had no idea what lay ahead. He knew he'd come through for Wayne, that the boy standing in front of him would take that man's place for a while, be it a day or a week. What did it matter, in the end? It would be like having Dillard back as a DHI, the momentary easing of the loss, the pain.

Beyond the door lay sunshine and joy and the wonder of Disneyland. What else mattered? What else even came close?

"I've figured it out," Philby said proudly.

"Let's hear it," Maybeck said.

"The letter isn't just for Wayne. It's for us, too. It's a Stonecutter's Quill or a Keeper Quest or some Wayne-ism that's going to explain everything." Philby was beaming, his face brightened by an inner light. Finn was relieved to hear he wasn't the only one; Philby was on board now, too. "Do you know what he's done? What we've done? Like Finn said: the impossible. If we turned around now, it would be like Columbus getting back aboard the ship the moment he touched the beach. The astronauts staying in their capsule and never climbing down the ladder onto the moon's surface."

He stopped, met their eyes one by one. Each Keeper. Young Wayne. Friends, old and new and . . . old.

"Are you kidding me, guys? We're going to get this close and not go through that door? Why go through all of this if that's the case? What's the point?" Philby answered his own question, still steadily smiling. "Wayne told us. He told Finn. He let us know what was going on way before we had even a hint. We turn around now, we'd be fools."

"Not that we can turn around," Maybeck said beneath his breath. "I'm just saying."

"What do you mean, he told us?" Willa asked Philby.

"Yeah!" Charlene echoed, incredulous.

"Seriously?" Philby exclaimed.

He and Finn met eyes. The pulse of brotherhood filled both boys, that feeling that comes only from completing an impossible task together. Then Philby nodded, deferring to Finn, as if to say: *You tell them.*

Finn nodded back. He looked down to see the faintest of images still lingering on his forearm: Walt's pen.

In a voice of hushed reverence, he uttered the words, the only words that made any sense.

"It's about time."

And as one, the Keepers turned to face the door.

CONGRATULATIONS TO THE KINGDOM KEEPERS INSIDER WINNERS:

Music_Vision Rachael Elmers
Abandoned_Wishes Mitchell Krueger
President_Escher Alissa Cook
Dark_Robinswood Kaelyn Marble
Stonecutter_Cannon Clayton Jarrard
Ladder_Finn Emma Marx
Wind_Princess Emily Tonne
Lost_Technology Nolan Gunsolley

Don't miss the next adventure:

A KINGDOM KEEPERS NOVEL

THE RETURN

BOOK TWO

LEGACY OF SECRETS

READ AN EXCERPT

1

OPENING THE DOOR

FINN WHITMAN HELD THE DOOR for Charlene. A gymnast and high school captain of three sports, Charlene now had her telltale sun-streaked blond hair in tight curls, her eyelashes clumped with mascara, her full figure crammed into an aqua-blue-and-white summer dress with a crinoline skirt, white bobby socks, and black flats. Her girl-next-door face was caked in makeup.

Girls in high school had hated Charlene for her looks. But those who actually spoke to her, who took the time to get to know her, liked her. What would those same kids think now? she wondered. High school was three months in her past; the world beyond the door was a full sixty years in the past—1955. She laced her transparent fingers in front of her like a bridesmaid to keep her hands from shaking.

Her four friends about to follow her through this same door were time travelers—just like her. They'd been part of her life since seventh grade. That was when she'd auditioned and been picked to be one of the human models for computer-generated holograms that would serve as personal guides through Disney World theme parks.

Finn addressed the remaining three teens. "We don't know what form the Overtakers will take, or if they even exist in 1955, so stay alert."

"And remember," said Philby, the redheaded boy at the back of the line, "our holograms aren't even holograms. They're two-dimensional, low-res projections that will barely fool anyone. So keep moving and don't stop to have conversations. This is dangerous ground, people."

The five Kingdom Keepers had little opportunity to contemplate the strange set of circumstances that had delivered them to this door. Their collective focus was instead on several things, all at once. 1) They were currently in 1955, a time they knew little about; 2) their mission was to locate and steal a fountain pen owned by Walt Disney; 3) the creative legend, Disney himself, was alive on July 17, 1955, and therefore somewhere in Disneyland, just beyond that door.

As it turned out, so were seven thousand news reporters from around the world, a camera team from ABC TV, hundreds—perhaps thousands—of Disney Cast Members, politicians, VIP dignitaries, and guests. Anaheim, California, had never seen anything like this. Today would change the course of history for the small orange-growing agricultural community. The Kingdom Keepers, being from the 21st century, knew all this. They were alone in this knowledge, as they prepared to crash the grand opening. If they failed to retrieve Walt's fountain pen, and find a way to ensure its discovery (by them!) six decades hence, then years of battling the

Disney villains, including the death of two close friends, would all have been for nothing.

"You'll have about twenty minutes," Wayne said, joining them at the door. "Mr. Disney's naps are very short, and he has a terribly busy day today."

Wayne was a few years older than they were—nineteen or twenty. They knew him better as a man in his eighties; a mentor; their advisor and confidant. Time travel was tricky.

"Napping?" Willa asked. Though Willa lacked the striking looks of Charlene, and the confident brashness of Philby—she was dark-haired, a little wide in the face, and reserved by nature—she had the brains of a wizard, the mind of a mathematician, and the calm of a lab scientist. "We're going to pick his pocket while he's napping?"

"It's the best opportunity you'll have," Wayne said. "Mr. Disney keeps his pen in the inside pocket of his sport coat. He won't sleep in the coat, so unless one of you is an expert at pocket picking . . ."

"We've got this," Finn said. "No worries." He had every worry, but wasn't about to put them on display for all to see.

"That's way too cheerful, Witless." Terry Maybeck seldom withheld his opinions. He claimed that, as an African American kid interested in art, he'd always felt sidelined, bullied, or otherwise ignored. His parents had either abandoned him or died; he didn't talk about it. He'd been raised by a bighearted aunt who ran a pottery shop. She claimed that Terry had been a head taller than any other kid in his class since the third grade, and had been spoiled by all the attention his teachers gave him, and because of this, had never been shy about sharing his thoughts.

"Thanks for that, Maybeck," Finn said. "Charlene . . . let's go!"

Once they were out in the park, everything looked and sounded so different from the park they knew. The five holograms moved through a Cast Member entrance leading from backstage into Town Square.

"What's weird," Maybeck said, "is how completely different something can look."

"I hear you," said Philby.

Sapling trees surrounded Town Square. Grass sod had been laid, but it looked more like green carpet. Flowers had been planted in neatly organized rows in front of stubby bushes. Only a few of the flowers held blossoms, which contributed to the naked look of the place. The park had the feeling of a model of Disneyland, not the real thing. Even the people were strange, in their white shirts, white dresses, and fancy shoes—the hair-sprayed hairdos of the women, the men's greased haircuts; everything about everyone was so intentional and perfectly in place that it looked more like a wax museum display than a day in Disneyland.

"Listen to them! They speak so differently," Charlene whispered to the others. "What's with all the 'gee whiz' and 'gosh'?"

"Don't look now, but it's 1955. 'Heck!' and 'Darn it!' are the closest they get to swearing. And look, they behave so differently!" Willa said. "Did you see that man tip his hat to that woman? So formal and polite."

A pair of burly men dragging television cables into place gave Maybeck an unpleasant look.

"I have a feeling," Finn said, "that they probably believe differently as well!"

Disneyland had more of a weekend carnival feel than that of a theme park.

"This is way cool, by the way!" Maybeck said, ignoring the men. "We get to see the original Disneyland!"

"See?" Professor Philby repeated, questioning him. Philby, always playing the academic. "Maybeck, we're not just seeing it, we're living it."

THE SLEEPING GIANT

The five Keepers had once helped to restore the Disney magic in Disney World by using Walt's pen to draw on an old blueprint of the park. That transformation had reversed the darker magic of the Disney villains—the Overtakers—and had launched a long string of successful battles against their dark forces. Their purpose here in 1955 was to find the correct pen and make sure it would be in the Disney Hollywood Studios attraction One Man's Dream, so that they could find it again fifty-odd years later, in the future.

As the moment approached, the five began moving

in eerie resemblance to a well-rehearsed team of bank robbers or street thieves. Outside of the Disneyland firehouse, alongside the Emporium, while the four teens stood side by side, a fifth, Finn, moved through a solid gate. Finn, whose boyish charm had matured into an intriguing forbearance. He had wildly expressive, almost hooded eyes, a mane of brown hair, and square shoulders that added up to a kind of Knight of the Round Table look of nobility. Now he found himself in backstage Disneyland.

It was nothing like the backstage Disneyland of the future. Carpenters, artists, craftsmen, and people from the television broadcast were so busy they were talking, walking, and banging into each other all at the same time. It looked like the world's busiest airport on the busiest day of the year. There were other inconsistencies: the sawhorses were wood, not plastic; the workers wore suspenders and heavy leather boots—not a running shoe to be seen. Not a single sports cap, either. These guys wore tams and berets.

Everyone smoked; cigarettes dangled from lips, were pinched between fingers. Unlit cigarettes were tucked behind ears, along with yellow pencils. There was not a bottle of bottled water in sight, nor aluminum cans. Finn saw some Coke bottles—greenish glass—a few glass milk bottles, and metal lunch boxes in the shape of small barns. Finn moved toward a carport that held four shiny new golf carts. As he did, his DHI projection sparkled and flared like a flickering TV signal during foul weather. Once at the carport, his image stabilized.

Next through the wall was Willa, followed by Charlene and Maybeck. At last, Philby's flickering projection came backward through the closed gate like a ghost.

"No matter how many times I see that it still looks so strange," Maybeck said.

"I hear you," said Charlene, equally awed by the metaphysical element of the projected holograms in action.

The five quickly split up, taking positions relevant to the scaling of the gray-painted staircase, which rose nearly two stories to an unassuming set of casement windows and a nondescript door. Charlene moved down the backstage lane and took up a guard position. Maybeck stood sentry at the bottom of the staircase, prepared to buy his friends time. Willa, Finn, and Philby moved their ghostlike projections through the metal chain strung across the staircase as a barrier. They climbed the stairs quickly, with as much confidence as they could muster. Moments later, they slipped through the exterior back door that led into Walt Disney's family apartment.

Each Kingdom Keeper had learned over the years to discipline his or her thoughts and to control his or her emotions. Everything they believed, everything they felt, affected the quality and abilities of their projections. Fear instilled limits; no fear opened up possibility. Entering Walt Disney's apartment uninvited while he was supposed to be napping felt criminal to each of the three. It took every ounce of confidence and patience they'd learned over the past few years to keep their composure.

Philby, the most analytical of the five, showed little outward reaction. Willa, who in high school had excelled past Philby in some academics, was less courageous. She looked ready to melt into the plush carpeting underfoot. Finn wanted to project confidence while not seeming pushy. He found himself the unofficial leader of the Keepers, but was occasionally challenged by Philby for that role.

The three communicated by hand signal. With everyone "talking" at once, it looked as if they were trying to flap their wings to fly.

When Willa slapped her hand over her mouth and stifled a squeal, Finn spun to see a fully dressed man asleep on the short red couch, his dress shoes indenting the armrest. Finn stared in awe. He'd seen so many videos, photographs, posters, and statues of Walter Elias Disney that seeing him in the flesh seemed so otherworldly he couldn't move.

Walt Disney snorted and began snoring softly.

Willa relaxed her hand. Philby placed his projected arm around her, and she leaned her head against his projected shoulder. Finn stuck his projected finger down his projected throat, indicating how he felt about the touching moment between the two. Philby stuck out his tongue and then laughed silently.

Finn took in the many items and pieces of furniture in the apartment, noting the differences between the real apartment and the restored version sixty years hence. Foremost was the brass fireman's pole mounted through a hole in the floor. The artwork on the walls was different as well: more photographs, fewer paintings. A suit valet stood by the end of the couch that wasn't there in the present.

As planned, Philby and Willa searched the closet. Finn inspected the suit valet and Walt Disney's sport coat, which hung there. The valet tray held U.S.-minted dimes, quarters, nickels, and pennies unlike any Finn had ever seen. The dollars clasped inside a silver money clip looked fake—in small letters they read "Silver Certificate." Finn reached to look inside the suit jacket, but his hologram hand passed through the fabric.

The easiest way for him to achieve the materiality that would lend his projection human substance was to allow fear into his thoughts. But that was risky—once mortal, he couldn't move through walls. Worse, weapons or fists wouldn't pass through him—they would injure him. Equally important: once fear sank its talons in and took hold, not only was it sometimes impossible for Finn to find his all clear projection again, but any harm that came to him in this condition would linger.

Leaders, Finn thought, didn't sit around thinking and stewing. Leaders led. He allowed himself to think about trespassing and attempting to steal something from one of his personal heroes. If caught, he'd be mortified.

If caught, then fifty-odd years into the future, there would be no pen to save the Magic Kingdom. The Disney villains known as the Overtakers would face one less obstacle in their objective to crush the Disney magic.

Finn's body tingled. He knew the feeling well: he was losing all clear. He was going mortal. Allowing it to grow stronger—warmer—he waited for the pins and needles to excite his fingertips. At that point, he fingered the fabric of Walt Disney's sport jacket, and the jacket came open.

A knock came from somewhere behind him. Finn froze, the fountain pen within reach.

The sleeping giant stopped snoring and startled awake.

Unwanted Words

Willa and Philby, in the midst of conducting a blind search of the few clothes hanging up in the dark closet, heard a knock. They paused. A second knock. "Maid service!" Another knock.

Philby stepped toward the closet door, but Willa held him back. Anxiety stole most of the all clear from her projection. She placed her ear against the cool door, catching the voices mid-conversation.

"I'm telling you, if Mister H says there's something here, then there's something here."

"And we're going to steal it?" said the other, her voice edged with uncertainty. Both voices were female;

both sounded young. "Golly, Gina! Doesn't that seem wrong?"

Mr. H. . . . Hollingsworth? Was that right? Willa wondered. A Dapper Dan, a Cast Member named Ezekiel Hollingsworth, had followed her and Philby through the park back in the present day. It had taken Philby some work to uncover the man's last name. But in 1955, Ezekiel Hollingsworth couldn't have been more than a few years old—if he'd even been born! So what Hollingsworth were these two talking about?

Trying to focus wasn't easy. As with the others, Willa had a great deal on her mind. How college was likely to separate her from Philby, whom she liked a lot. How the best years of her life seemed destined to come to an end. How friendship was like some kind of puzzle: just when you thought you understood it, there turned out to be deeper, undiscovered levels.

Willa had kept her excitement to herself when Finn proposed this final effort to recover Walt's pen. Secretly, she'd been brimming with joy. This would keep the five of them together, even if it was just for a few moments longer. Her thrill at being in Disneyland on Opening Day was like sunshine wanting to burst from behind a cloud. Everything was clean and fresh, like a brand-new house whose front lawn hadn't grown in yet. She wanted to dance her way down Main Street.

One of the women spoke. "Remember: anything unusual. A wand, in particular."

Willa heard the instructions, but her mind was back

on the name: Hollingsworth. What could a man sixty years in the future have to do with Opening Day at Disneyland?

"You hear that?" Willa whispered to Philby.

"His snoring stop? You betcha I did!"

Willa wanted to correct him, to explain what she'd heard the maid say. But he was right: Walt's snoring had stopped. Finn!

"Right," she said, trying to remain calm. "We'd better get out of here."

PENNY PINCHER

Finn had just taken hold of the suit coat's lapel when the napping Walt Disney rose up on one arm. He looked in the direction of the knocking.

At that moment, Willa and Philby stepped through the closet door and into the narrow hallway behind Finn.

With Walt distracted, Finn focused and directed his prickling fingers to the valet's tray table. His first effort to pick up one of the pennies failed. But he pushed, gathered his full concentration, and managed to make himself solidly physical enough to manipulate matter. In an instant, Finn had flung the coin towards the small table at the window looking out onto Town Square, which held a replica gas lamp. The coin clinked as it landed.

The groggy man whipped his head toward the sound.

Finn peeled open the sports coat, snatched a

fountain pen, which had been clipped inside the chest pocket, and headed for the back door, a step behind Willa and Philby, who moved, ghostlike, through the solid wood. Finn clutched the pen tightly in his hand. As a material object, it wouldn't pass through the door like his projection. He was reaching for the dead-bolt lock when an eerily familiar voice called out, "Hello?" It was a voice Finn knew from DVDs and YouTube. It was as powerful to him as the Wizard was to Dorothy.

It was Walt Disney.

Finn dove for the fireman's pole. He slid down the brass pipe and landed on a hissing cushion shaped like a doughnut. Except for a single silhouetted figure standing in the open bay door, the firehouse stood empty.

Finn tried to catch his breath. The air was hot and smelled of sawdust and pine. Being a projection, Finn didn't actually breathe, but to him he felt he did. If you asked Finn Whitman, he sweated, breathed, ached, and itched, just like his human, solid self. And he maintained that illusion. By agreement, the Keepers kept their projections secret. There would be far too many questions to answer if found out. Now he just needed to get past this man without incident.

"And just where did you come from?" the man's thin, almost cartoony voice asked. It had no place in one so tall and formidable. Finn wanted a better angle, a chance to see the man's face.

Finn had to think quickly. "I run errands for Mr. Disney. I'm an errand runner."

"Is that so?"

"I like taking the pole. Makes me feel like a fireman." Even without seeing the man clearly, Finn could tell he didn't believe him. He could think of several reasons why that might be the case—first and foremost, Finn was a lousy liar. But another possibility was that the man had expected someone else to come down the pole.

Finn heard the muted sound of feet coming quickly down the stairs. The silhouette heard them as well. The stairs led to Walt's apartment, but Willa and Philby—who wouldn't make clunky sounds—should have already made it down.

"Mr. Hollingsworth!" the voice of a young woman called. The man spun. Finn saw his face in profile: a Roman nose and cleft chin, wide eyes—brown?—and big ears. Plain looking, not handsome, Finn thought.

The name meant something to Finn—he'd heard it from Philby, maybe.

Hollingsworth shot a final look in Finn's direction. Though he remained silent, something shouted to Finn: "Watch yourself!" Then Hollingsworth turned and caught up to the two young women, both of whom were dressed in maid uniforms. The three vanished into the overwhelmingly thick crowd.

Feeling threatened and afraid, Finn ran for backstage. He couldn't get there fast enough.

It would be the last Finn ever saw of the two girls.